Pretending

Aria Gomez

Contents

CHAPTER 1 :Meeting Him

"Come on try it on " said Brie, I let out a small laugh at her facial expressions.

Brie is my best friend, I have known her since high school, I don't know what I would do without her.

" Okay fine but only if you stop making that face" I said trying to stop laughing. She threw the red dress at me and I went to try it on. It was really tight but it made my ass look good so that's great,I looked hot. I put on some makeup and perfume.

"Come on hurry up we're going to be late! " Brie shouted from downstairs.

"Coming" I shouted down scrambling to get my heels on.

"Finally" she said exhaling when I came down a few moments later.

"Okay let's go "I said nervously.

When I say I'm nervous, its an understatement, I've never been to a club before and I wasnt planning on ever going because it's just horny men who want mindless hook ups and they don't ever want to see you again.

We arrived at the club a while later and Brie must've seen me being so tense.

"Loosen up its your birthday and guess what... We're going to have a fucking great time.. We're going to go dancing and we're going to drink till we can't remember anything tomorrow."she said chuckling with her hand on my shoulder.

" I know thanks Brie" I said putting my hand on her hand.

" Whats the worst that can happen" Brie said shaking her head.

"Let's go" I said exhaling and getting out of the uber. Brie and I linked arms and went in the club.

What's the worst that can happen I suppose. I only turn 25 once might as well live it to the fullest.

We ordered some drinks but I was hesitant because I have never had a drink in my life but I'm trying new things so I might as well.

We got shots of tequila, Brie swallowed the three without any hesitation, while the tequila is burning my throat. "Come on, let's dance" she said dragging me to the dancefloor.

Imagine this song playing..

https://www.youtube.com/watch?v=n2fEUGtLhIQ

"Okay, let's go"i said.

We danced for what felt like ages, the music was so loud it was vibrating through the floor and there was disco lights and smoke clouding the room.

" I'm going to get some drinks okay,"!Brie said shouting through the sound of the music.

"Yeah I'm going to go to the bathroom" I said close to her ear so she could hear me. "We'll meet at the bar okay" I said, Brie nodded and left to get the drinks and I left to go to the bathroom.

It took me a few minutes finding the bathroom but I finally found it. I did my business and went back out to findBrie, I went to the bar as that's where I said to meet because there is like a thousand people in here.

She wasn't there when I got there but I'm sure she's just talking to someone or making out with someone,I waited for a few minutes, but I was starting to get worried so I texted her.

Brie, where are you, I'm by the bar?

She texted back a few minutes later,

Hey Vic, gone home with some guy, who is so hot, I'm sorry for bailing I'll make it up to you tomorrow or something. Love you Vic, don't forget to have fun it's your birthday!! Okay talk to u tmrxx!!

I smiled and texted back sitting down on a stool beside the bar.

Okay it's fine you need it stay safe and plz call me tmr love you have fun xx

I'm happy for Brie, even its only a one night stand, she deserves a good time as she went through a bad breakup a few months back,he was her first love type of thing but I think she's over him now.

"Hey you, here's a drink" I looked up from my phone to see the bartender handing me a drink.

"Umm I didn't order anything, I said confused.

"Yeah I know he did,"he pointed to some guy across the room and man he was hot. He was wearing a black suit. I made eye contact with him, I got butterflies by just looking at him, I was so busy staring I didn't notice him walking towards me.

" Hello, love"

CHAPTER 2:Hello Love

"Umm, hi, thanks for the drink, but you didn't have to, I can buy my own" I told him.

"Your welcome, I just wanted to get a drink for the beuitaful girl who's sitting alone. " he replied.

"Well thank you for the drink" how is he so hot.

"May I ask what your name is? "he asked with his hands in his pockets.

I smiled at him." My name is Victoria, what's yours. "

" Let's keep that a mystery"he said, I smiled at him and picked up the drink and drank it, it tasted like shit but I disguised it with a smile.He smiled back before talking again.

" Have a good night, Victoria I'll see you soon " and then he walked away.

God he was the hottest man i had ever seen. I exchanged a few glances with the mystery man and I got butterflies everytime we made eye contact.

I stared him for a while longer but I was starting to feel drousy so I gave him one last glance before leaving. Maybe it's the drinks finally getting to me. I went outside, and the fresh air felt so good.

I called myself an uber, and waited. As the minutes went by I felt like I was going to faint and I did not want to faint right here as anyone could kidnap me and do god knows what.

I walked towards home and I was almost there as I lived like 10 minutes from the club. I looked at my phone to go cancel the uber and it hadn't even moved. It was still at its starting point. Self note :never call for an uber again.

I can't wait to get inside and go to bed, my dress Is practically suffocating me right now and my feet are sore from walking in these heels. I feel like shit right now. I saw my house and I practically ran to the door. I stumbled side to side trying to get my keys out of my purse but I couldn't find them.

I see a van pulling up a few metres from me and some guy came out dressed in all black. He looks really creepy. I rooted through my bag some more until I found my keys.

I put them in the door trying to open it but my legs fell out from under me, I fell to the ground and the last thing I saw before darkness consumed me was the man coming over to me and picking me up and putting me in the van.

https://www.youtube.com/watch?v=TaA9RWkUaYo

CHAPTER 3:Taken

Today my mother told me I should get married and settle down and have a family, but that's the last thing I want I just want one night stands with women and never see them again.

I was bored as fuck and needed to get out of the house so I decided to go to my club 'The sin'. When I got there I was swarmed with women but they were all ugly as shit.

"ACE brother "someone shouted calling me over, it was felix

Felix is my brother.

" What are you doing here?"I asked him.

" What do you mean it's my brothers club and come on and its full of hot chicks", he said waving his hand to all the women in the room. We talked about our mother wanting me to get married.

"Just get married it doesn't have to mean anything, you don't have to love each other, get married and divorce a few months later and tell mom it didn't work out and she'll get off your fucking back." he said leaning back into his chair smoking pot.

"It's not that easy Felix, you know her she'll just want me to get married again." I said.

He laughed, "It is that easy, just look at all these women just find one you like, pick her, offer her money and get married, done simple as that.

I groaned before swallowing my shot of tequila in one go.

I looked at the dance floor to see if any of them was to my liking.No one was. I looked at the bar, beckoning the barman to get me another drink,and I saw the most beautiful girl. She was In a tiny red dress.She was sitting down by the bar. I saw her and some other girl talking. They talked for another few minutes before going to the dance floor.

I watched her and her friend dancing.

"See anyone you like" Felix asked.

"Yes" i moved my head to where she was dancing.

"She's hot, so's the girl she's dancing with, I'm just getting horny looking at her, he said.

" Can you not go a day without being inside of a cunt? ", I asked shaking my head.

My love said something to her friend before going to the bathroom.

" I can but I won't", Felix said before getting up and going dancing with the friend.

Not even two seconds later they were kissing each other. Felix whispered something to her and she nodded. He came over to me.

"It's that easy bro, talk to you tomorrow." I rolled my eyes.

"Yeah OK bye and be careful, call me tomorrow" I said to him and he nodded. They practically ran out of the club. Kids these days.

My love came back from the bathroom and went over by the bar. She was looking around for a few minutes clearly waiting for her friend but she was gone.

She went on her phone and I could see she was upset so I ordered her a drink but I put something in it that will make her sleep for a few hours.

I gave it to my barman and told him to give it to her. He gave the drink to her and she started talking with him. He pointed at me and we made eye contact. Her eyes are like the ocean.

I almost smiled but I composed myself. I decided to go up and talk to her. She was still staring at me when I got to her.

"Hello, love." I said to her.

She snapped out of trance before answering,"Umm hi thanks for the drink, but you didnt have to, I can buy my own" she said.

"Your welcome, I just wanted to get a drink for the beuitaful girl who's sitting alone" I replied.

"Well thank you for the drink", she replied.

"May I ask what your name is "I said putting my hands in my pockets.

" My name is Victoria, whats yours?"

Victoria, such a pretty name

" Let's keep that a mystery" I said, she smiled and downed her drink. Good girl.

"Have a good night Victoria, I'll see you soon ". I left but I payed close attention to her. We glanced at each other for a while but drugs were starting to take affect because she got up and left. I told my bodygaurd to follow her. A few minutes later I got a text from him.

I have her. She's knocked out like a light.

She's the one, she's the one I'll marry. Your mine now love.

https://www.youtube.com/watch?v=EIGbAnIQb-M

CHAPTER 4:Unlucky

I began to wake up, and thought about how I got here. The mystery guy who wouldn't tell me his name must have drugged me.

"Hello, love" he said. I jumped up from my lying position and stared into his eyes.I remembered how he was so sweet last night,it was too good to be true.

"It's you "I said." Your the guy from last night, what did you put in my drink."

" You remembered" he said. "I put a pill in your drink that would make you sleep for a few hours, it's safe don't worry your fine."

"Who are you and why am I here" I asked.

He smirked before answering, " My name is Ace de Luca, love."I stared at him blankly for a moment and then realised who he was. Ace de Luca is the leader of the Italian mafia.

I heard about him a few months ago he killed an entire gang because they stole drugs from him. Dramatic I know.

"Do you know who i am" he said.

"Yes I do now please tell me where i am" i saidholding my head from the throbbing headache I had."You are in Italy love" he said to me.What. "What do you mean I'm in Italy, why am I here, why did you take me"!

"You will find out soon enough, love" he said before standing up and leaving.What the fuck??

2 hours later

After crying for 2 hours and looking for away out, which I couldn't do by the way, I'm locked in this room and I'm on the top floor so I can't exactly jump off the balcony.

I was bored and so I went to look around the room incase I could find a weapon and throw it at Ace for when he comes back so I cna escape.

I couldn't find anything, there was just soaps in the bathroom that was it, I suppose I could throw it at his head and try to run.

I picked it up just incase the opportunity came to me. I looked in the bathroom mirror and I looked like shit. My hair looked like a mop, my makeup looked like shit and my mascara was all over my face from crying.

After a few minutes of exploring the room i finally heard a door open And I hid behind the bathroom door and had the soap in my hand ready to throw.

I heard footsteps come towards the door but before they could come any closer I threw the soap at them and it hit them in the face. It was Ace.

I didn't wait around for his reaction and I ran past him but he tried to grab my wrist but I was gone, I guess my running skills aren't as bad as I thought.

I raced down the halls looking for somewhere to hide, but I saw the stairs and ran down them,I could hear Ace shouting something but I couldn't hear him.

His guards were now running after me trying to get me but I was too fast for them , I reached the bottom of the stairs and saw the front door and I ran to it and opened it.

I ran out the door and was now in the garden, there was a driveway so I tried getting to that as it must lead to a road. Ace's men were running towards me but I swerved half of them, right when I thought I was getting away someone came in front of me and I tripped, but luckily I didn't hit the ground.

Before I could do anything they lifted me up and put a cloth to my face. The person turned me around so I could see their face and it was him.

Ace

"I really wish you didn't do that, love" he said.

I tried to move my face away from the cloth but it was no use. I fainted into his arms. The last thing I remember was him picking me up bridal style and saying" Don't worry love, I got you. "

https://www.youtube.com/watch?v=F7k4Tm59dsg

CHAPTER 5:Ace

After talking with Victoria I went to my office. I was meant to get in a shipment of drugs yesterday but I never got them. I was pissed off.

"MASSIMO, GET IN HERE NOW!!"

Massimo entered the room.

"Yes boss "

"Where are my drugs I was meant to get them yesterday?!"

"I don't know there might be a delay I will check now."

"Well find them,i need them here by tomorrow".

"Yes boss"he said before leaving.

I'm even more pissed off then I was yesterday. I need to see her again. As I go into her room I didn't see her. She must be in the bathroom so I went towards the door, but I got hit in the face with something.

She then ran out of the bathroom and I tried to reconsole myself after getting hit in the face. I tried to grab her wrist but she too fast. Fuckin hell.

One of my guards came down the hallway and I shouted GET HER DONT LET HER GET AWAY!! I swear to god they were all useless.

I went downstairs myself and went out the door. She was still running across the lawn, obviously trying to get to the road, but little did she know the roads a mile away. I chuckled a little from all the chaos she has caused in the space of the 24 hours she has been here.

Half my guards were after her and not one of them could catch her. I had to do this shit myself.

I walked up in front of her, she couldn't see me as she was looking behind to see if the guards were close.

She came closer and I tripped her. I caught her before she hit the ground. I put her facing away from me and put a cloth to her face, this should make her sleep for a few hours. Before she faints I want her to see me and show her how pissed off I am.

"I really wish you didn't do that, love"

And she was gone.

"Don't worry love, I got you." I said and I picked her up and brought her back to bed. I put her in the bed covered her with the blanket.

I picked up the soap that was on the ground and put it back in the bathroom.

I went into my office because I had a shit load of work to do. Massimo better come back with some good news or I swear to god.

A few minutes later Massimo entered the room.

"I found your drugs boss, they will arrive tomorrow." he said string down in front of the desk.

" Good, thank you Massimo. "

"No problem,"he replied. He got up and headed toward the door.

" Before you leave, we have an invitation to the Revera ball tomorrow night so we need full security,"i said.

The Revera's are the New York mafia. Our families are good friends and we meet up every few years to discuss business.

"Yes boss I'll get that sorted, goodnight."

Goodnight, "I replied.

I will bring Victoria and introduce her to everyone and make everyone believe that we are a happy couple madly in love and about to get married.

How hard can it be.

https://www.youtube.com/watch?v=fczTADY1v3I

CHAPTER 6:Victoria

I woke up to the sound of someone entering the room. It was a maid.

"Miss, here is your outfit for tonight go to the shower and get cleaned up and I will help you get ready".

I got out of bed and stood up.

"What do you mean outfit for tonight am I going somewhere, am I going home?" I asked hopefully.

"Yes, you are going to a ball tonight with Mr de Luca. I'm sorry your not going home but here is your dress for tonight.

"What do you mean I am going to a ball. I don't want to go I want to go home. Can you help me please. "

"Im sorry miss but I can't I will get into trouble if I do just please go to the shower. "

It was pointless so I just said "Okay" as I didn't want to get her into trouble.

I'm not gonna lie the shower was amazing it felt so good. I stayed in for a good 20 minutes and tried out all the soaps. I shaved and got out. It felt so good to be clean.

If I'm going to a ball I could ask someone to help me. There will be alot of people there I could easily slip out unnoticed. I need to get out of this shit hole. I need to see Brie and let her know I'm OK.

I got out and dried myself and went into the room. The maid was there.

"What's your name" I asked her if I'm going to be here for longer then I want I need to make a friend.

"My name is Aubrey miss. "

"That's a lovely name. My name is Victoria. "

She smiled. "Let's get you ready then." She did my makeup, hair and she put on my dress too. I told her I could do it myself but she insisted.

I looked in the mirror and I looked so different. Normally I would only wear foundation and mascara.

These images are the dress makeup and heels and hair.

I looked so different. I wish Brie could see this. She always wanted me to get out of my comfort zone. I miss her so much. I need to escape fro here and I'm going to do It tonight I have to because it's the only chance I have of getting my freedom.

"I think you look lovely miss."

"Thank you for helping me get ready"

"No problem miss, Mr de Luca will be here in a few minutes."She then left the room.

"Okay".I sat down on the bed and started thinking of how tonight's gonna go. I needed to escape and fast.The door opened a few minutes later and Ace walked in.

He was wearing a black suit. I got butterflies just by looking at him but remembered the fact he is holding me here against my will.

THIS IS WHAT ACE IS WEARING.

WITHOUT THE TATOO.

"Are you ready" he asked. I nodded and stood up and walked towards him, he held out his hand and I took it.

This is going to be fun...

CHAPTER 7:The Ball

The ride to the ball was super awkward. Me and Ace didn't say anything to each other, but I liked it that way, it gave me more time to think about what I'm gonna do when we get there.

I could try and get away from Ace and ask someone for help.

I just know I need go home, I have to find Brie because she's all I have. My parents died when I was 5 years old, and my older brother Elijah left 5 years ago when I was 18 and I haven't seen him since then .

He was 21 when he left me and I have no idea where he is.I miss him so much, I hope I will see him again one day.

"We're here" Ace said with a tone. I looked over at Ace and he was back to his usual self he looked annoyed, Well it was nice while it lasted.

A man came over and opened our doors. "Thank you" I said and he smiled and walked away. I looked at the house and It was incredible.

It looked so nice. There was a pool with water coming up from it, I was so in awe of the house I didn't realise I was smiling.

"That's the first time I've seen you smile since Ive met you " Ace said to me.

"Well you kidnapped me and drugged me two times." I said back to him.

"Yeah I suppose that's fair". He held out his hand to me wanting me to take it. I was reluctant to take it but I did. When we went inside of the house it was even more beautiful.

"ACE IS THAT YOU!", Some man shouted and came over and shook hands with Ace.

"I dont believe it, it's been ages since I last saw you", he laughed at ace.

"I've Been very busy with the mafia" Ace said to him.

"Yeah I suppose, buissness these days right" he winked looking at Ace.

He then looked at me "Who's this beuitaful young women" he asked.

"My name is Victoria nice to meet you".

"That's a lovely name, my name is Lucus nice to meet you too", Marianne come over here and see Ace and his girl".

I tensed up as soon as he said that , I could tell Ace did too as he had his seriously pissed off face on. I ignored him and looked at Marianne, she walked over and kissed Lucus on the cheek before looking at me and Ace.

"Hello Ace it's great to see you again and who's this " she asked looking at me.

"This is Victoria" replied Ace.

"It's lovely to meet you Victoria my name is Marianne."

"Its lovely to meet you too" ,I replied.

I wonder if Lucus is in the mafia too.

"Well we better get going we have other people to see and buisseness to discuss, "he winked at Ace.

He's totally in the mafia too. Shit. My plan has gone to shit. I will have to think of something else and fast.

When Lucus and Marianne left, Ace and I went to the ballroom, there was a huge table with champagne, wine and fruits. There was waiters going around to everyone with drinks. Everyone looks so intimidating.

I need to find a way to get away from Ace. I can say I'm going to the bathroom or something. I will do it later because the party is only starting and he will get suspicious If I go now.

Music started playing and everyone joined up together and started dancing.

"Come on dance with me, love."

I hesitated but I said "Okay" and linked arms with him.

https://www.youtube.com/watch?v=ShYd8KzTG7E

We joined the dance floor with everyone. Ace took my hand and put his other hand around my waist and I felt his cold touch vibrating through my body,I put my hand on his shoulder and we danced to the music.

"You still haven't told me why you took me" I said staring into his eyes.

He didn't say anything for a few seconds but just stared into my eyes.

"Well your about to find out, come with me", he said taking my hand and leading me down a hall and into a room.

"Why are we in here." I asked getting a little scared.

"Well, I have to tell you why I took you and I thought I should tell you In private."

" Okay so tell me" I ordered nervously.

"I need you to be my wife, " Ace said calmly.

CHAPTER 8:Ace

"Fuck!!" I shouted,I was in my warehouse and I was pissed off I had some unfinished business with an enemy of mine and found out he is going to be at the ball tonight. This enemy of mine is named Lorenzo, he is the leader of the Nigerian mafia.

Tonight is going to be good for me and Victoria, everyone will know I'm with someone and that will set my plan In motion, but I'm going for another reason, I'm going there to kill Lorenzo and his mafia.

L

orenzo has caused alot of problems for me over thr last few years.

Years ago when I was 18 years old Lorenzo sent his men to kill my father as he saw that this mafia was a threat to his. He did kill my father and I became Don of the Italian mafia.

I didn't care that my father was dead because I hated him, he cared more for the mafia then his own family. BUT no one messes with my family and gets away with it, Lorenzo will pay for what he did.

I need to go home and shower before the ball. I had blood all over me from killing two men for the unfortunate problem with my drugs.

After a cold shower I put on my black suit,then I went to see Massimo to make sure everything was ready for tonight.

A few minutes later

"Yes boss, everything is ready to go. Your security team is blended in with Lorenzos" .

"Ok thank you massimo good job and get the cars ready to go we will be leaving soon ."

Everything's going according to plan.

"See you soon boss". Massimo said before leaving the room.

I sat down at my desk and went through some paperwork. I got a text from Felix. Finally. The fucker hasn't texted me back in days.

Felix 5:32pm Whats up brother been busy the last few days but Im going to the fancy ass ball later too so we can talk.

Ace 5:34 Where the fuck have you been I've been calling you for days. Yeah we will. I'm killing Lorenzo tonight he is going to be there too. I have everything ready to go.

Felix 5:37

Count me in too. See you there bro.

It's time to get Victoria, I hope she's in better mood today, If not my plan to persuade everyone we're together won't work. I walked to her room and opened the door.

There she was in a black dress where you could see all her curves and it hugged her body perfectly. She looked hot. I was just getting hard by looking at her,but then I remembered this is not part of my plan.

"Hello, love".I spoke in alow voice. She looked at me and her body grew all tense. I love how she reacts when I'm near her.

"My name's Victoria so stop calling me that". She spoke rolling her eyes. I smiled at her confidence, she spoke back to me, a mafia leader, no one ever dares to speak back to me

"Okay i'll try but I can't promise anything". I said to her still smirking.

A few minutes later

On the ride there I could tell Victoria was uncomfortable but I liked it. I was looking forward for tonight,I can't wait to kill Lorenzo and his entire mafia.

After I tell her she's going to be my wife I don't know how she will react but she's going to have deal with it.

Life isn't fair sometimes.

CHAPTER 9: The Bombshell

I stared at him in disbelief. I even laughed a little. If he thinks Im going to be his wife he's more phychotic than I thought.

"Why are you laughing.I'm being serious" he said sounding angry. He crossed his arms and you could see his rings and his veins on display.

"Your crazy if you'd think I'd be your wife you kidnapped me, drugged me and your holding me against my will, your a monster, why would I ever marry you".

That was it, within a blink of an eye he marched over and pushed me against the wall and put his hand on my neck and squeezed so hard that I couldn't breathe.

"Believe it or not love I don't want to be in this situation either but guess what, life isn't fair sometimes ", he said. He was so close to my face, I could feel his warm breathe on my face.

He looked me right in my eyes and smiled at the pain he was causing me almost like he was enjoying it.

"Please, Ace let go your hurting me. "

Tears were running down my face at this point. I was in so much pain that I felt like I was going to pass out.

Ace let go of my neck and I fell to the ground and clutched my neck gasping for air. Ace stood there and watched me and didn't show any emotion.

" You are going to be my wife and that's final."

Ace left the room and I just curled up in a ball and cried my eyes out and lied there on the cold office ground. My mascara was running down my face and my makeup was probably ruined but I wasn't thinking about that right now.

10 minutes later

I just layed there crying thinking about everything and what I could have done differently. Why did I have to go out, maybe if me and Brie went to a different club things would have been different.

All of a sudden I heard gunshots and screams. I stood up faster then ever and went to the door and it was locked. Ace must of locked it when he left but I mustn't of noticed.

I need to get out of here now. I grabbed one of the clips from my hair. My hair fell loose but it doesn't matter. I put the clip in the lock and moved it around and unlocked the door. When I opened the door Ace was standing there and he had blood all over his shirt with a gun in his hand.

There was blood splattered all over his face. I looked at him with wide eyes and I got flashbacks of what he did to me a few minutes ago.

"Come on we're going now and follow me or don't that's up to you, you can get killed if you want I don't really give a shit." he started walking down the hallway putting his gun in the back of his pants, and I followed him.

When we got outside I saw the rest of Ace's mafia and people were running out of the house and people were driving away. What the hell is going on??

" ACE what's going on?"I ask scared.

Ace turned around from talking to his bodyguard, I think his name is Massimo.

" Nothing you need to worry about, this is Colin and he is going to take you home, wait for me to get back I'll be done here soon ", Ace said gesturing to one of his bodyguards.

"Yeah Okay" I replied.

"Good",Ace said before whispering something to Colin.

Colin led me to the car and he drove me home, we didn't say anything to each other but I looked at him a few times because he looks so familiar and I don't know why, but I don't think I've ever seen him before.

Finally we arrived back at the house.

We got out of the car and walked inside.Colin left as soon as we got inside and I went upstairs to get out of dress and I went to the bathroom to take off my makeup and saw that I had a massive bruise on my neck from Ace nearly strangling me to death.

I was hungry so I went downstairs to make some food for myself.

A few minutes later Ace walked through the door, he still had blood all over him but it was gone from his face.

"What are you still doing up?" he asked.

You told me to wait up for you and I was hungry so I made some food Umm... do you want some, I made pasta?

I don't know why I'm offering him food but he looked hungry so I thought I'd ask.

"You do know I have maids for that right."

"Yeah I do, but why ask them to cook for me when I know perfectly well how to cook" .

He groaned and sat down in front of me. I served him a bowl of pasta and handed it to him.

"Thanks" he said, before eating.

I sat down and started eating aswell.

Ace looked at my neck and his gaze softened.

"I'm sorry I hurt you, I shouldn't have done that and I won't do it again" he said.

I put my hand to my neck and replied" Thank you ".

When we were done our food I washed the plates and put them away.

" Goodnight Ace" I said before going upstairs.

" Goodnight" he said following me.

"We will talk tomorrow"he said before disappearing into his room.

I whispered"OK" before going into my room.

CHAPTER 10:The Deal

When I woke up I put on some clothes and went to get something to eat.Ace was there.

"Goodmorning" I said

"Morning" he replied getting something out of the fridge.

"You said we were gonna talk, so let's talk."i spoke sitting down on the chair.

" Yeah we will but I have buissness to attend to for the day so we will talk later when I get back. "

" What will I do just stay here for the whole day?".

" No you will go shopping I'm sure you need some new clothes, Colin will take you.

Shopping.

" Yeah okay thanks. I do need some new clothes."

"Good and we will discuss everything when I get back." he said.

"OK thank you Ace. "

He gave me an intense stare and then walked away. I made some breakfast and went to the shower and got dressed to go shopping. I put on jeans with a crop top and a warm cardigan.

I cant wait to get out of this place and see people. Normal people.

I waited downstairs until Colin came.

"You ready to go" he asked

"Yeah I am" I replied.

"Okay let's go then". I nodded and we left the house. On the drive there I just looked out the window and thought about what Ace Is going to tell me later.

I already know he wants me to be his wife but why. Why me?

"We're here "Colin said.

We went around the shops and I picked up some cute outfits. Colin followed me but stayed a little behind me.

A few hours later I was done shopping and we went home, Ace wasn't there yet so I went up to my room to put away my clothes.

A few hours later I was watching TV in my room and there was a knock on the door.

It was Audrey.

"Miss,Mr de Luca will see you now" she said.

"Okay thanks Audrey" I replied. I got up and went to his office and knocked on the door.

"Come in", I heard from the other side of the door.

I went in and Ace was sitting there with his sleeves rolled up and leaning back into his chair.

"Hello love "

Hi" I mumbled back.

"Did you want to speak to me", I asked sitting on the chair in front of his desk.

"Yes we need to talk about our marriage" he said.

"OK" I responded.

"We will be married for six months and then we divorce, that's it. I will pay you, just name your price" .

"What? You want us to get married for six months.Why?" I asked.

He groaned as he leaned back into his chair. "My mother wants me to get married and I'm doing this so she will get off my back, I will tell her the marriage didn't work and we divorced and you will go back to your life and I will go back to mine.

" So wait we just have to get married for six months and that's it."

"Yes, that's it" , he said.

"What If I don't want to get married to you, will you let me go now."

"No I won't I will kill you".Ace said smirking.

Great.

"Okay fine, I'll marry you it's not like I have any other choice."

"Good girl, now sign this"he said passing me a sheet.

" What's this" I asked confused.

"It's a contract, it tells you everything you need to know."

The contract just said that we have to get married for six months, get divorced, and never see each other again.

I'll be able to go back to my life, like nothing ever happened.

"So do we have a deal.. Wife."

I stared at him for a moment before replying.

"Yes we do... Husband" .

I guess I'm getting married.

CHAPTER 11:Unexpected

I guess I'm getting married...

"We are going to go for a picnic tomorrow just you and me. We can get to know each other. "

"I wouldve never thought someone like you would want to go on a picnic" I smiled and chuckled.

"You don't know me yet, love. I can do things you wouldn't dream of."

"As we are going to be married we will be sharing a room" he said.

"Why? "I asked.

My mother will be coming in a few weeks and we need to make it believeable."

"Okay fine. "

We need to make it believeable in order for this to work, if his mother suspects something is up, he could kill me.

"Come on I will show you our room".

"Do you like it" he said leaning against the doorway with his hands in his pockets.

"Yeah I love it" I said smiling.

"Good it's yours for the next six months".

An hour later.

I didn't do anything for the next hour I just had dinner down in the dining room by myself because Ace had to go do some buiseness.

It was 10:00 and was tired so I went upstairs to my room and went to go put on something. I couldnt find any pajamas. The wardrobe had everything in it accept pyjamas.Great. I looked around and saw one of Ace's shirts and put one on. It went down to my mid thigh. I climbed into the bed and turned on the huge TV. I watched Netflix for a while then I turned it off and tried to go to sleep.

An hour later Ace walked in and I woke up . He went into the walk in wardrobe and he came out in grey sweatpants and climbed into bed behind me.

He wrapped his hands around my waist and pulled me in so close I could feel his breathe on my neck.

I could get used to this...

https://www.youtube.com/watch?v=6wJEEcTIPss

CHAPTER 12:Ace

It's been a long week with everything going on with Victoria and the marriage contract.

After we talked about the contract i had to go out and deal with shit as per usual. Someone is causing problems down in my casino and I'm going to blow their head off. I don't like problems so I deal with them.

When I got to the casino there was people running out. I pulled up beside thr casino and ran into it with my gun in hand. When I got in I saw someone who caused a lot of problems for me years ago but I could never find him but here we are. The fucker doesn't know this is my casino what a surprise.

"Long time no see Nikolai "I said walking towards him.

He turned around from thr bar with a drink and a gun in his hand.

He stared at me confused and then his eyes opened wide when he remembered me.

" Ace"?

"I guess you remember me then. Now can you tell me why you are in my casino causing all these problems for me. "

He started thinking of what to say."Im sorry ace I didn't know this was yours.... Uh my wife just left me and I'm upset okay.....Please don't kill me just let me go....please."

I started laughing. "I'm not surprised Elizabeth left you."

"I'm sorry ace just please let me go and you will never see me again" he begged.

"No Nikolaii" I sighed "You've known me for a long time and you know that if anyone crosses me they die."

He got off of the chair and got on his knees and started begging.

"Your pathetic you know that". I shot him in the head and he fell back. My guards came running in adn went over to the body.

"Clean this up" i said to them all and I walked out and went back to my car and got in and went home. I needed to see my love.I wonder if she's asleep I hope not Im hoping we can talk more about our little arrangement.

When I got to the house I went to the shower downstairs in another spare room because I didn't want Victoria to suspect anything as I had blood splattered all over me.That's the last thing I need right now.I ate something because I was fucking starving and hadn't eaten dinner.

After I ate I was tired so I went upstairs to go to bed.After the shower

I changed into my grey sweatpants and snuck into the bed beside Victoria.

I have never had a women in my bed before, I never let anyone sleep with me.

I got into the bed and I grabbed her waist and pulled her into me and feel asleep.

The next morning...

When I woke up she was still in the same position and fuck she looked so hot. I could feel the boner forming so I moved my arms out from under her and got up and went to the shower.

After relieving myself I got out of the shower and went back into the room. Victoria was there on her computer watching Netflix. She looked up at me and smiled.

"Goodmorning, wife.I said to her while smirking.

She shut her computer and looked back up to me. "Goodmorning, FUTURE husband ", she said smiling.

Her smile... Fuck.

I smiled at her." Get ready we are going for breakfast" .

Maybe this way we can talk more because I have to get to know her more as she is going to be my future wife after all and.

"Really, okay" she smiled at me and got out of bed and went to get changed.

CHAPTER 13:Ace And Victoria

☐ Warning

When Victoria was ready we went in my car. She looked beautiful too.She was wearing a sundress, it fitted her perfectly.

This is what Victoria is wearing.

Im bringing her to a cafe my friend Laura owns,she's my friend Matthews wife and he is also a mafia boss,he is the mafia boss of Spain but they are here in Italy for business.

"Where are we going "Victoria asked me .

" We are going to a cafe, I heard they have good food " I replied.

I pulled up beside the cafe and turned off the engine. I got out of the car and went to open the door for my love. I'm going to get to know her a lot better today.

When she got out I took her hand and we went inside.

" ACE Is that you" said Laura walking towards us.

"Hello Laura, this is Victoria my future wife."

"Lovely to meet you Victoria, I'm surprised he has someone he's such an asshole. "

Great.

Victoria smiled at her and I squeezed her hand tighter as I could tell she was nervous. I can read her like a book.

"Can we get some breakfast please Laura. "

"Yeah no problem I'll bring you your menus take a seat and I'll be there in a second. "

I brought Victoria over to the table and she let go of my hand and sat down beside on the chair beside me.

Laura came over and gave is the menus.

"So when's the day your getting married. "

She stared at me smiling. I swear she can be a bitch when she wants to, she's doing this on purpose too.

"We don't know yet we are terrible at making decisions aren't we love". I put my hand on her thigh and she tensed up straight away.

She smiled." Yeah we are. We just want to take our time and make sure we really think about it."

"Okay well I'll be over in a few minutes when your ready to order."

Sitting there with Ace so close to me Is stressing me out. He still had his hands in my thigh and I could feel how warm his hand is. It's igniting a feeling in me and it feels good. Its like a pulse beating in my core.

When breakfast arrived he still didn't take it away.

"Anyway tell me more about yourself love ". He said to me while raising his glass of water and drinking it.

"Umm.... My name is Victoria but you already know that...umm.. I'm 25 and both both my parents are dead umm they died when I was younger."

When I said that he looked at me with a sad face almost like he felt sorry for me.

"Sorry to hear that," he stroked my thigh.

"It's okay I was young I don't really remember them anyway.I also live alone and I'm a nurse aswell. "

"What" I said smiling at him.

"A nurse huh"

"Yeah it's always been my dream job".

" Ace what are you doing?" I know what he is doing but we can't do this here, especially in public even though there's only a few people in here but it's still public.

His hand was moving sideways now moving towards my inner thigh and moving upwards until I could feel his hand touching me.

"Do you trust me love?" He asked. "No"I swallowed my mouth dry."I don't." He smirked. "Good"

He leaned over and whispered "Even if you don't trust me I think you want me to do this,i can already feel how wet you are and I haven't even touched you yet love."

" I don't know what you mean." I said back to him quickly. Fuck I'm not doing it on purpose, body why are you betraying me right now.

He still had his hand on me and he began stroking my underwear but I could fell his finger against me and fuck I was so turned on right now. I tried to move but his other hand stopped me.

"Do you like that, love" he said smirking at me.

I didn't say anything back I was just focused on his fingers that are moving my underwear out oh the way. My eyes widened and I immediately went to grab his hand but his hand went on top of mine. He leaned in and whispered "Trust me love you'll love it no one's watching us".

He still held my hand and continued moving my underwear out of the way. Fuck this is so embarrassing but fuck it felt so good.

He put his finger in and moved in and out I put my head on his shoulder this feels so good. He put another one in and moved faster. I let out a small moan I was so close to have an orgasm right now but I can't.

"Do you like that love I can make you scream my name so the whole world knows your mine and you will be mine". I came all over his fingers and he took them out and put them in his mouth. Wtf is he doing. Ewww.

"Delicious love". He fixed my dress for me and kissed my forehead.

"Let's go I have buisseness to take care of" he said while putting cash down on the table.

"Okay. "I got up from the table

" Thanks Laura."

" No problem bye Victoria lovely meeting you."

"Bye thanks you too." Ace took my hand and we walked out.

What the hell just happened and more importantly why did I allow him to do that to me?

https://www.youtube.com/watch?v=fwqe3Yf4Iqo

CHAPTER 14:Brie

As we were going home I thought about everything that just happend. He literally fingered me. It was my first time doing anything that intimate. It felt so good too. I have never had that feeling and I want it again and i feel guilty because of it.

When the six months are up and I can forget about him and never see him again.

All I know is that I can not fall in love with him.

I can't wait to see Brie again, I miss her so much.

"What are you thinking about" Ace said to me bringing me out of my daydream.

I'm fine just thinking about my friend Brie.

Can I call her, I have to let her know I'm ok "

"He waited a few seconds before answering" Okay fine but you will be supervised I don't trust you yet and I don't want you to.... try anything."

"Okay thank you."i smiled at him and turned to look out the window again.

I didn't care that I would have to be supervised I was just so happy. I can't wait to hear Bries voice again. I hope she's okay.

When we got back to the house, Ace and I went to his office. I signed the contract and went to my room, he left to go do some business, I didn't care about anything else I was just so happy I get to call Brie. Ace said I can call her when he comes back.

While waiting for him, I decided to go to the shower, I stayed in there for ages the water felt so good against my body. When I got out I put on some jeans and a crop top it looked really short but It looked nice so I put it on.

I went downstairs and got something to eat since I hadn't eaten for a few hours. While I was eating Ace came in the front door with someone.

"Victoria this is Felix" he said to me and walked up and sat down.

"Hello Victoria I've heard so much about you, I'm his brother. "

"Hello Felix nice to meet you" I replied back to him. He seemed more different compared to Ace.

He hugged me and then he went upstairs.

I sat down beside Ace and stared at him.

"So can I call Brie... Please. "

He turned his head and looked at me. "Yes you can call your friend but if you try anything I will kill you do you understand".he stared at me with his grey eyes. If looked could kill I would've been dead a long time ago.

"Yes i do thank you." He handed me the phone and I jumped up from the chair and hugged him. I didnt realize what I did until I did it. I let him go and ran up the stairs.

I was going to call my friend and I felt so happy.

CHAPTER 15:Family

As I dialled Bries number, I began to feel nervous and i don't know why I wondered what she might say and how she will react to all this.

I've known her since high school and we became best friends straight away she stood up for me when I was being picked on by an older kid and we clicked straight away and it's been the same ever since.

When I dialled the number I got up from the bed and started pacing around the room.

What if she doesn't answer,what if she thinks I'm dead.

Finally she picked up.

"Hi, who am I speaking to"she asked in a bored matter.

"Brie, it's me Victoria" I replied sitting back down on the bed.

"Victoria is that really you,oh my god where are you are you okay!?"She shouted into the phone sounding worried.

"I'm okay Brie, really I am. I'm in Italy."

"BITCH! What! Your in Italy" she shouted into the phone.

I started laughing, i am so glad to hear her voice again.

Yes" I replied laughing.

"Tell me everything,Im getting a plane ticket and I'm coming to get you, its been a month since I had heard from you last, why didn't you call me and let me know you were okay I thought you were dead Vic."

I felt so bad at how she must have been feeling the last months.Tears starting appearing in my eyes.

"I'm so sorry Brie I really am. I don't know if I would be able to see you if you came. The night we went out someone took me and brought me to Italy and I've been here ever since. Look you can't come here Brie, he could kill you he's a very dangerous person."

"Well I'll be a dangerous bitch myself I am going to call the police and they will come and get you okay, and they will arrest the pervert who took you . You're going to be okay Vic I promise."

I love her so much. I felt so guilty for what I was about to say next.

"As much as I want to come home Brie I can't, and you can't call the police Brie okay promise me you won't" .

"Why not?"Brie snapped back.

"He's Ace de Luca Brie the Italian mafia leader"I said to her. There was silence on the other end for a few seconds before she replied.

What" she said in a low voice.

I was full on crying at this stage and I could hear sniffles on the other end of the call I think she was crying too.

"Yes Brie he's a mafia leader which means he's very dangerous okay so promise me you won't call the police, If something happend to you I could never live with myself. "

"Okay, I promise. Are you okay is he hurting you."

"No I'm fine I really am he's not as bad as I thought he was we've gotten closer over the last few days. I just really miss you."

" That's good then, I'm surprised he let you call me" she said with a giggle at the end.

I sighed." I know me too but I made a deal with him. I have to be married to him for six months and then when the six months are up we will divorce and go our separate ways and never see each other again. I know its a lot to take in "i said when all I heard was silence.

"Why did you do that Vic?

"I had no choice I had to sign the contract and if I didnt he said he'd kill me."

" Okay Vic just promise me that you are safe and that you will call me everyday to let me know your okay. "

" I promise I'm okay Brie, I promise I will call you everyday."

I didn't know If Ace would let me do that but I didn't care It just made me happy to think about talking to her everyday but I'm not going to think about that right now.

We talked more on what she's been up to for the last month and we laughed about everything.

There was a knock on the door and Audrey came in. She whispered "Dinner is ready" and I nodded and then she left. I looked at the clock and it was 5:32.I had been talking to Brie for more than an hour.

I really wanted to keep talking to Brie but I didn't want to push my limits.

"Brie I have to go okay dinner is ready but I will call you tomorrow I promise".

"Okay I will talk to you tomorrow. Vic you have no idea how good it sounded to hear your voice again."

"Me too Brie I love you talk to you tomorrow."

"Okay Vic, love you too bye. "

I hung up the phone and went downstairs smiling. I was so happy Ace let me call her, maybe he isn't as bad as I thought he was.

Little did Victoria know is that I was listening to her conversation the entire time. One thing I know now is that I can trust her.

Perfect.

CHAPTER 16: The Special Day

T he wedding

A week later

Today I'm getting married to the most dangerous man in Italy. I was in my room and Aubrey was helping me put on my dress.

The dress

"Are you okay miss, "Aubrey asked me with a concerned look. I was looking in the mirror looking at myself and I was so nervous just a few months ago I was normal and now I'm getting married to someone I know nothing about. I turned to look at her she was standing behind me with a worried look.

"Yes I am, just nervous that's all I'll be fine I'm promise." I shook off the nerves.

Let' do this. Its only 6 months and then I'm done and I will never have to see him again.

"Miss you have to go now" Aubrey said to me as I was waiting to go down the aisle.

"OK thanks Aubrey". Okay here we go.

I smiled at her one last time and sighed. Let's do this.The first thing I saw when walking down the aisle was Ace, he looked so bitter I couldn't tell if he was angry or happy. We made eye contact and I held my bouquet tighter, we held eye contact until I got to the aisle,I broke the eye contact and handed my bouquet of flowers to Aubrey.

I turned back to face him.

"Hello, love. You look beautiful. "

"Thank you" I replied.

A few minutes later

"You may now kiss the bride"

Shit.

He leaned over and got closer to my face. I closed my eyes waiting for the feeling of his lips on mine but it never came. I opened them and he stood there just staring back at me.

"Come on let's go" , he started walking down the aisle.

What

I followed him and we left.

In the car I just looked out the window. How could I be so stupid. I actually thought he was going to kiss me.

"When we get home get changed we're going out to one of my clubs I have buissiness to take care of so be good".

A club fucking great he can go fuck himself and his club.

"No thanks ill stay home".

He sighed.

"That wasnt a question love just do as I tell you and we won't have any problems."

" Fine", I sighed and just played with my ring.

Victoria's wedding ring

When we got back to the house I went up to my room as soon as I could. I would do anything to go home and hug Brie right now. How did my life get so shit.

I went to the closet and picked out a nice dress.

When we got to the club there was loads of people there.

"Stay by the bar I have some business to take care of, "he started walking but turned around...

"And don't try anything "

I nodded. He left, I went over to the bar.

"Can I get three shots please" I asked the bartender and sat down on the chair. I looked around to see if I could see Ace but he disappeared. I drank the shots and went dancing I was drunk but I didn't care Ace can fuck off with all his demands. This marriage isn't real and never will be. I danced to the music for a while then Some guy came up to me and put his hands on my waist and started grinding against me.

This is the song playing

https://www.youtube.com/watch?v=LtM_IjQ6nlw

I didn't care that some stranger was grinding against me, we stayed dancing with each other for a few minutes, "My names Ryder" he said to me.

"Ryder that's a nice name mines Victoria nice to meet you." I replied smiling.

"That's such a hot name", "he replied before he started kissing my neck,that will definitely leave a mark.

All of a sudden I could see Ace coming down the stairs he couldn't see me at first I was frozen I couldn't move. He was looking around with a very angry looking face and then we made eye contact. Fuck,I'm dead.

He pushed through the crowds and got to us in a blink of an eye. By this time Ryder stopped kissing my neck and loosened his grip around my waist.

ACE stared at me blankly before turning to him.

"IF you ever lay hands on my wife again I will cut them off."

Ryder left and before I could say anything. Ace grabbed my hand and brought me upstairs to a room, I'm guessing he owns this club too why am I not surprised.

In the room there was a bed and a couch. Fifty shades of grey vibes...in a club...

He let go of my hands and practically threw me in the room I fell on the bed because I'm drunk and just sat there waiting for him to give me a lecture.

He locked the door behind him and turned to me.

"What the fuck do you think your doing Victoria hmm are you trying to make me angry."

" No I just wanted to have some fun and you weren't there."

"If I wasn't so angry I might be tempted to fuck you right now, "he said

Two can play this game.

"Then do it" I said getting up and walking towards him.

His eyes widened a little and went to get a drink from the table. He then sat down on the couch.

"Don't patronise me, Victoria. "

I walked towards him and sat down on his lap and started to straddle him.

He put his hands on my waist keeping them from moving.

"Love, what are you doing, don't start something you can't finish."

"What does it look like I'm doing, I.. Want... You... To... Fuck.. Me," I said while straddling him.

I honestly don't know what I'm doing but I honestly Dont care.

He stared deeply into my eyes before kissing me with force, he was fighting to get into my mouth with his tongue and I allowed it.

He grabbed my ass and stood up I wrapped my legs around his waist while he walked us to the bed.

He layed me down on the bed gently before undressing himself and I began to unzip my dress. I kicked off my heels and was only left in my bra and knickers. He was left in his underwear.

He admired me for a few seconds before getting on the bed and kissing me, he unclipped my bra and threw it on the floor and started kissing my breasts and sucking on my niples, I let a small moan out but covered my mouth.

"Don't do that love I want the world to hear you scream my name and know that you're mine and only mine. "

He started kissing downwards and reached my underwear, he took them off and threw them aside.

He started kissing upwards and reached my lips and started kissing me again.

"Are you sure you want to do this love."

I nodded. I really did want to do this. I'm really losing my virginity to him and it feels so right. He reached over me and grabbed a condom from the bedside table and pulled down his underwear and put it on.

He massaged my clit for a few seconds.

"Your already so wet for me love. "

Before I could say anything he pushed himself inside. It hurt so bad. I closed my eyes.

"Are you okay love we can stop if you want,"he looked at me with a worried look.

"No I'm fine keep going", I reached in and grabbed his neck and pulled down, I kissed him and he went a bit faster and the pain started to go away I moaned into his mouth and he groaned too.

"No one could ever make you feel like this, your mine and only mine say it. "

I grabbed the sheets and closed my fist. I could feel him on my core and I was so close to having an orgasm.

I looked up at him.

I'm yours".

"Good girl", he kept going faster and I was so close, "Come for me love" , I obliged and came all over him and he did too, we kissed each other while we released. We let go of each other and he fell on the bed and layed there. We were breathing loudly over the sound of music from downstairs.

He took the condom off and put it in the bin. He began to get changed and I just lay there.

That felt great, it wasn't how I imagined it would be.

All of a sudden there was a knock on the door.

"Boss there's a problem downstairs" someone shouted

ACE groaned before replying"Okay ill be there in a minute. "

He grabbed his drink from the table and swallowed the last bit of drink he had left.

"Get changed love we're leaving soon" .

What your leaving... Now". Why am I not surprised he's arrogant and impulsive.

"Yes there's a problem downstairs now get changed or I will dress you myself."

I stared at him for a while longer. He started walking towards me and I got up quickly.

"I can dress myself", i got up from the bed and grabbed my clothes.

"Then do it I'll be up in a few minutes... Be ready when I come back. He unlocked the door and left me In my thoughts. I got changed and sat on the bed, waiting for him to come back.

What have I done...

WARNING

HELLO EVERYONE I HOPE YOU ARE ENJOYING 'PRETENDING TO BE HIS'.

THE NEXT FEW CHAPTERSARE CONFUSING..THEY ARE BUNGLED IN DIFFERENT SECTIONS SO LOOK AT WHAT CHAPTER YOUR READING FIRST.

THE CHAPTERS GO 19, 20, 17 AND 18

I DON'T KNOW WHY THIS IS HAPPENING I TRIED TO MOVE THEM WITH THE TABLE OF CONTENTS BUT IT WOULDNT WORK.

SORRY FOR ANY CONFUSION THAT WILL BE CAUSED...

THANK YOU GUYS FOR READING.-KAYLEYCONSI

CHAPTER 17:Shopping

Over the next few days I avoided Ace as much as I could which was easier than expected. I made sure to fall asleep before he came to bed.

We haven't talked much since the wedding and I liked it that way. How could I have been so stupid to fall for his charms. I lost my virginity to someone who doesn't care about me. He probably fucks alot of girls.Im not surprised though i mean he is hot which would make anyone fall to their knees.

Today is Saturday and I just woke up.I got up and went to the shower and got changed into jeans and a nice top.

Im going to go shopping today to buy some new clothes, I badly need them. On my way down the stairs I'm thinking of what I need to get. I need sanitary towels and makeup remover.

I stop up on the middle of the stairs. Wait,im late. I havent had my period in a while. I can't be pregnant because we used protection. I just shrugged it off and continued down the stairs, it's probably late because of the stress but I'll pick up a pregnancy test just to be safe.

Ace's keys were on the table so I picked them up.I will just go shopping myself, I'm Ace's wife now so I should have a bit more freedom and I can't exactly run off because he will find me.

I saw a notepad and pen on the table so I wrote a note to Ace so he wouldnt be that mad at me.

Gone shopping be back later. -Victoria

I grabbed the keys and left. When I got outside i went to the lambourghini and got in.

Sweet ride, this is going to be fun.

I've been very busy the last few days and I haven't talked with Victoria since our wedding night and I don't like it. I don't do this. I'm not used to it. When I spend the night with a women I plan on never seeing them again. I only do one night stands that's it.

I wasn't planning on feeling anything for her. I wasn't planning on getting this close.This was just business.I felt a connection with her when we had sex. I never felt that way before.

"Boss"

I looked up from my papers to see. Massimo standing by the doorway.

"What do you want Massimo I'm busy."

He stood there with an expression on his face that made me want to punch him, I don't need any bullshit today.

He smiled Trying not to laugh"Your wife has taken one of the cars, she has gone shopping, she left a note on the table for you."

What, why can't she just behave for one fucking day.

Why wasn't anyone watching her!!"I let out a breathe I had been holding in for a while. " Massimo I swear to god she better come home safely or else".

So far my shopping experience has been great, I got some new clothes that I can't wait to wear.

I went to a pharmacy and got my pregnancy test too, it was really expensive even though there's just one of them in the box.

I had coffee at a nice café and decided to go home as Ace will kill me if I'm back any later.

On the way home I was thinking what if I am pregnant. I'm not ready to have kids yet but if I am I will give my life for my baby and I will always protect them.

When I pulled up in the driveway it was really quite, maybe nobody has noticed I'm gone yet.

When I got out of the car I got my bags and went inside. No one was there.

I set my bags down and went to get a glass of water. I then heard someone storming down the stairs. Let me guess, Ace.

"Where the hell were you "he asked standing with his arms crossed showing all his veins.

" Shopping" I pointed at the bags and put my glass of water down on the table.

He looked at the bags and then looked back at me,"And who said you can leave the house... hmm do you not remember the rule where you can't leave without my permission."He looked at me with a very serious and angry face.

Okay I'm dead

I sighed before answering," Okay I'm sorry I left the house without your permission I won't do it next time, but you can't expect me to stay here for six months and not go anywhere "

" If you want to go anywhere you have to go with me or with one of my guards that's final."

I crossed my arms and leaned against the countertop.

" Okay fine"

"Good.... Look Victoria about the other night.... I "he stammered then stopped and looked up at me. I stood up straight and went a bit closer to him. It's weird I've never seen him being this...... Vulnerable.

"Were you going to say something? "I asked hoping he'd bring up the wedding night and everything that happened.

" No, forget it" , he started walking towards the stairs and turned around.

"And don't go anywhere without my permission, I won't let you get off that easy next time."

And old Ace is back

"Yeah okay" I smiled and he went upstairs again and I grabbed my bags and went upstairs too.

https://www.youtube.com/watch?v=URh38mzcU9c

A few minutes later

After putting all my bags on my bed ready to sort them out I remembered my pregnancy test.I took it out of the bag and looked at it.

Okay let's do this.

I went to the bathroom and when I was done I put the test on the counter top and I sat on the edge of the bath.

A million things are going through my head right now.

What if I'm pregnant? What will Ace do when he finds out? Would he be a good father to our child?

I waited for 3 minutes and went to look at it. I sighed before turning the preganacy test over.

Negative

I'm not pregnant. Okay I suppose that's a good thing, I'm not ready to be a mother and Ace definitely isn't ready to be a father and besides when the six months are up it will be like this never happend and I will go back to my normal life.

I got changed into my pajamas and put the test under my clothes in the closet. Ace won't look through my things and I'll get rid of it tomorrow. The last thing I want is for him to find it and start asking questions.

I put on the TV and watched it for a while before I fell asleep.

CHAPTER 18:Who Will Protect You

☐ Warning

I was so close to telling Victoria how I felt and I can't allow myself to feel something for her. I can't be vulnerable because it's the biggest weakness of all. I won't allow myself to be weak,not again,not what happend last time.

I went back up to my office and went through some paperwork. I got sent word that I am going to war with the Vinsenzo mafia, they are the Spanish mafia. That mafia was Lorenzos rival mafia, but they signed a deal a few months back. Now that I killed Lorenzo and his entire mafia that deal won't happen, now they want to kill me.

A while later Massimo came into the office.

"Have you figured out what to do yet boss?" he asked me.

I leaned back into my chair," No I haven't, I don't know why the hell there coming after me, I killed that bastard a month ago.. so why now? I need full time security guarding the house and Victoria,I can't let anything happen to her."

Massimo looked at me with a surprised look on his face.

" Why? Are you falling for her boss"?

I gave him a glare before replying.

"No, I don't love her and I never will. She is strictly buissness, this is only happening because my mother is so persistent in me getting married,But still I need to protect her at all costs." If anything happend to her because of me I wouldn't be able to live with myself, she is only here because I am forcing her she doesn't deserve to die because of that.

"Okay boss I'll make sure she has full time security " Massimo said.

"Good, now go I need to figure out what to do about those Spanish bastards" I said.

" Okay... Good luck with that haha goodnight "he said.

" Goodnight" , I replied, Massimo was laughing on his way out the door.

A few hours later

I went through all the possible solutions but I came down with one finally.

Victoria and my mother will go to my penthouse in Poland to keep them safe and I will stay here and go to war with the spanish mafia, I will Win of course because I am the most powerful and feared mafia. I have won a war before against the American mafia and I killed every single one of them, so I will win this one.

I will tell Victoria and my mother the news tomorrow. I don't expect Victoria will want to go but she'll have to,and as for my mother she hates being bossed around but she will know its for her own good.

It was 2 in the morning now and I was wrecked so I decided to go to bed. When I got to the room Victoria was asleep. She was huddled in under the blankets. I was so tired I just took off my shirt and pants. I wasn't bothered getting into my sweatpants.

I climbed into bed and looked at Victoria, she looks so beautiful. I removed the piece of hair that was in front of her face and tucked it behind her ear. I know I shouldn't have but I need her closer to me, I lifted her up and brought her to me.She laid her head on my chest and cuddled in.

I made a promise to myself and to her that I will never let anyone hurt her and I intend to keep that promise until the very end.

The next morning

When I woke up Victoria was still cuddled in to me. I stared at her for a while until she started waking up.

She saw that she was cuddling me and that her hand was on my chest. She looked up at me and we stayed there for a few seconds before I spoke.

"Hello love" , I smiled at her, still holding her.

"Goodmorning" she smiled before putting her head back on my chest.

I held her and looked at her, I need to tell her that she's going to Poland for a while but I know that when I do she's going to leave. Fuck it.

"Your going to Poland for a while with my mother. "

She sat up and faced me.

"What, Why? Is something wrong are you coming too?"

I sat up against the bed frame "No there is nothing wrong, I just have some buissness to take care of, but I want you to be safe so you will be going to my penthouse In Poland with my mother. You will be meeting her today, we are going to dinner with her this evening and you two will be leaving tomorrow."

"Buissness? What type of Buissness? "she asked.

" It's just mafia Buissness it's fine.You'll be safe if that's what's your worried about,thats why your going to Poland so I can protect you" . I said getting out of the bed and walking towards the wardrobe.

She got out of the bed too and followed me. "No I'm not worried about that I'm worried about you" she said to me while I was putting on my shirt.

I stopped what I was doing and turned to look at her.

"Well don't be, I've been in the mafia since I was 18 years old and look at me I'm still alive and I don't have a scar on my body"

She looked at me speechless."What, you've been doing this since you were 18? "

"Yeah, I took over the Buissness from my father when I was 18 because he became an alcoholic and couldn't do anything anymore." I said to her.

She came closer to me and hugged me. I was shocked but I put my hands around her waist and pulled her in closer to me.

" I'm so sorry Ace you didn't deserve any of that" she said.

"It's fine I hated him anyway" I replied.

She let go of me and looked at me and we stared at each other not saying anything, I still had my hands around her waist.

I know I shouldn't do it but fuck it I can't help it.

I kissed her and she kissed me back, i lifted her up and put her legs around my waist. I carried her to the bed and put her down before taking off my shirt. I kissed her again and my tongue was fighting to get into her mouth and she let me. Good girl. I took off her top and pants and she was left in her bra and underwear. She is so hot. I am so hard right now and I need her right now.

I stopped kissing her and leaned my forhead against hers. "Do you want to"?I asked and she nodded. "Use your words love." "Yes, ace i want you inside me, now" . I leaned over her and grabbed a condom from the bedside table. I ripped it open with my mouth and put it on.

I kissed Victoria and then kissed her neck and kissed down onto her chest. I took off her bra and kissed her breasts and sucked on her nipple, she arched her back and moaned. I smiled before kissing downwards and taking off her underwear, I pulled her to the edge of the bed and kneeled down.

I kissed her thighs and went upwards. She tasted so good. I got up and kissed her again.I slipped one finger inside and she moaned in my mouth. I put in another and she arched her back.

"I'm going to come ace, I'm so close."

"No don't come yet" , I said to her, I want her to wait.

I took my fingers out before putting my dick inside her. She let out a moan and wrapped her legs around me. I went harder and the sound of her moans filled the room, our flesh slapping together.

" Fuck Victoria" , I groaned." I'm going to cum ace" Victoria said between moans. "Then come for me love, come all over me" I said to her. We came at the same time and I kissed her again. I pulled out and leaned my forehead against hers.

I went back to our conversation before.

"Your going to be okay I'll protect you I will always protect you." I said to her still leaning my forehead against hers.

"I know" she said, "But who will protect you."

https://www.youtube.com/watch?v=3GQVhIfZq5A

CHAPTER 19:Meeting His Mother

- -

A ce and I are currently eating breakfast in the kitchen. I was thinking about what just happened,I know me and ace had sex before but this time it felt different.

"We are meeting my mother at the restaurant so act like you love me okay" . He said getting up from his chair.

What if I already do

I gave a smile, "Yeah, I know", I said getting up aswell.

You and my mom are leaving tonight, you will be leaving in my private jet after we eat.

My eyes widened "What Tonight? Why so soon I'm not even packed yet" . I asked crossing my arms.

"Don't worry about any of that, I told Audrey to pack your bag." He said leaning against the counter.

"How long are we gonna be gone for?"I asked.

I havent even met Ace's mom yet and now I'm going to Poland with her for god knows how long.

He closed his eyes and sighed.

" I don't know, you won't come back until everything is cleared up."

" Cleared up? What are you talking bout Ace. "

What the hell is going on.

"Don't worry about it Victoria,just go get ready I don't have time for this I have stuff to do before we meet my mother."

"No, not until you tell what's going on, why am I going to Poland and don't give me this "mafia buissness" bullshit because I know there's more to it" I said to him angry.

Before I could say anything else he stormed up to me and backing me against the counter.

"Don't you ever speak to me that way again. Know your place Victoria, we don't care about each other it's a show, for my mother, so when I say it's mafia business I mean it's mafia buissness okay and you are going to Poland because I don't want to get you killed because in a few months your going back to your life and I'm going back to mine, after all, this is what you wanted since the moment I brought you here so don't give me that bullshit, you are in no position to be asking me questions that don't concern you." He said a few inches from my face.

I pushed him away from me and walked away from him.

" Ace I'm your wife and I know this isn't real you remind me everyday but just tell me what's going on, when are you going to let someone in", i said to him with tears in my eyes.

"Just tell me please ace that's all I'm asking. "I pleaded with him.

He looked at me angrily before speaking.

"Go. Upstairs. Now." He demanded walking closer towards me with every word.

"Tell me what's going on please" . I begged.

"Get upstairs before I drag you there myself." he said right in front of me.

I wiped the tears that were falling from my eyes.

" Your going to be alone forever Ace", I said before turning around and going upstairs.

Why can't he tell me whats going on, I already know he's in the mafia and he kills people, how bad could it be. I wiped away the tears and got changed into my dress for this evening. Im meeting Aces mother so I have to look presentable.

I decided on a long black dress. I was feeling nauseous so I made sure not to put on something tight.

ACE came in while I was putting on my makeup in the bathroom but we didn't talk and he was only a few minutes getting ready.

When I was done I put on some perfume which made me feel even more nauseated which was weird but I shook it off.

When I got downstairs Ace was talking to someone, it sounded serious. It's probably about his "mafia business".

He gave me a quick glance eyeing me from head to toe and looked away. I rolled my eyes and went over to the sink to get a glass of water to get rid of my nausea, hopefully it will go away soon.

"Let's go", Ace said I washed my glass and put It down beside the sink and got my bag. I followed Ace outside and got in the car.

"My mother will be meeting us at the restaurant, so do you remember what you have to do". He asked staring at me.

I turned to look at him before saying" "I have to act like I love you".

"Good girl" . He smirked before bring his eyes back to the road.

"Does your mom know about Poland"?I asked,I wonder does she know whats going on.

"Yeah I told her earlier, she wasn't happy at first but then I told her you were going too, shes looking forward to meeting you. "

I smiled "Me too.

I don't want to get too close to Ace's mother because I won't be here for much longer. I only have 4 months left of this deal and then I'm going home.

I still felt sick but I was slowly starting to feel better.For the rest of the drive I layed my head against the car door because I was really tired and still felt sick I think my period is coming finally. I must have fell asleep because Ace shook me when we arrived at the restaurant.

"We're here come on" he said getting out of the car. I fixed my hair and dress and stood beside him on the footpath.

He held out his hand and we intertwined our fingers and walked in to the restaurant.

Let's put on a show..

CHAPTER 20:THE DINNER

As we were walking into the restaurant a million things were going through my head. What if Aces mother doesn't believe us. What's going to happen if she doesn't, will I ever be allowed to go home.

I squeezed Ace's hand for comfort.

"Ace!"i looked to see where the noise was coming from and I saw a women who doesn't look a day over forty, she must be Aces mother.

Damn she's aged well

We walked towards Aces mother and Ace let go of my hand and hugged her.

Hi mom its good to see you.

Yes it is now let me see your wife she said letting go of Ace and practically pushing him out of the way so she could see me.

She looked at me and her eyes lit up.

"Ahh shes gorgeous" she said before pulling me into a hug.

"My names Lucinda,ahh it's so great to finally meet you".

It's a pleasure to meet you too, I'm Victoria"I said smiling hoping I was making this as believable as I possibly could.

We stopped hugging and I went over and stood beside Ace. He put his hand around my waist and pulled me in closer.

" Me too sweetheart I have been dying to meet you, I'm sorry I couldn't come to the wedding, I'm so glad Ace has met someone, I can tell your an angel.

"Yeah she certainly is Ace said moving his hand a small bit lower.I smiled because I know what he is doing, but it quickly faded when I remembered earlier.I smiled at Lucinda and then looked at Ace.

"Can we sit down and eat because I'm starving" Ace said to Lucinda. Lucinda rolled her eyes and then Ace let go of my waist and started walking towards our table.

"It's so great to meet you, I couldn't wait to see the woman who raised Ace,you did such a good job, he's really great", i said to Lucinda while we were walking towards our table.

"Thank you sweetheart that means alot, after his father died it went downhill, I dont know if he told you about what type of father he was but he was never there for him or Felix and It really affected them, and of course I wasn't the best mother then either, and Ace had to look after me and Felix, but I can tell he is very happy with you so thank you for bringing my boy back to me".

I had tears in my eyes and I smiled and I hugged Lucinda.

"Now let's stop being emotional this is a happy time", she said as she grabbed my hand before walking towards our table.

I sat beside Ace who was restless looking at the menu and Lucinda sat in front of Ace.

After a few minutes we ordered our food, I got a chicken salad because I was still really nauseous.

Anyway Ace tell me more about Poland where are me and Victoria staying.

Ace sighed before replying."You are staying in my penthouse for a while and then your coming back when everything is sorted."

She nodded and left it at that. She must know not to ask questions, she probably knows he is a mafia leader, well of course she knows her husband led it first before Ace took over.

Our dinner arrived a while later and we started eating,but halfway through our meal I felt like I was going to throw up.

"Im going to the bathroom" I said getting up from my chair.

"Are you alright sweetheart" Lucinda asked.

I nodded"Yes I'm fine Im just feeling a bit sick I must have ate something bad."

" Oh sweetheart I hope your okay" she said with a worried look.

Ace looked at me too with a serious look. I left them and I practically ran to the bathroom and threw up all the contents I had eaten today. I took a tissue and sat on the toilet and wiped my mouth.

God what is happening to me

After Victoria went to bathroom it was silence. I hope shes okay she's acting weirder then usual.

"You should go and check on her sweetheart she's been in there for a while."

"I'm sure she's fine mom" I replied before putting food in my mouth.

I looked up to see my mother looking at me like I've done something amazing.

I swallowed my food before speaking."What? "

"Is she pregnant?"

My eyes widened at the thought.

"No mom she's not, I would know if she was."

She sighed in disappointment and sat back In her chair.

"When am I going to be getting grandchildren Ace"?

Jesus christ.

"I don't know, in a couple of years, Victoria and I haven't talked about that yet", I said hoping that would end the baby conversation.

I never want kids,with my mafia I can't have anything that could be used against me.Its dangerous enough having Victoria as my 'wife' let alone ever having children. After a few more long minutes Victoria still hadn't come back and even I was starting to get worried.

"I'm going to go check on her mom I'll be back in a few minutes." I said getting up from my chair.

"Okay sweetheart do, I will get the cheque."

I gave mom my credit card and she smiled.

"Your such a good boy Ace."

I rolled my eyes before leaving to find the bathrooms.

I still felt really nauseated and I couldn't leave the bathrooms yet. I must have the bug or something. A few minutes later I got up from the toilet and opened the stall door. I washed my hands and was about to leave when Ace came in.

"Ace what are you doing in here get out."

He locked the door so no on could come in. He gave me an intense stare before speaking.

"Are you pregnant?"

"What, why would you think that. "

"Because you've been in the bathroom for ages and you've been acting weird all day, so I'm going to ask this once and one time only Are you pregnant? And don't lie to me."

He started walking towards me and I stepped backwards, I was now trapped between him and the wall.

" I'm not pregnant Ace" I said nervously.

"Why don't I believe you" he said angrily.

I felt like I was going to throw up again but I held my stomach to make it feel better.

"I took a pregnant test a few days a go and it was negative, so can you relax now, I'm not pregnant.

" What why didn't you tell" me he said angrily

"Because I knew how you would react and besides like you have said a million times before, our relationship isn't real. Look I must have just eaten something bad or something. I'm sure that's all it is.

" Well it better be" he said before leaving the bathroom. I followed him and he was there with Lucinda.

When Lucinda saw me she smiled. "Are you alright dear you were in the for a while."

I nodded "Yes I'm fine I must have eaten something bad this morning" .

"Okay if you say so sweetheart."

I walked over to Ace and stood beside him.

"Are you sure your okay love" he said.

I forced a smile" Yes I promise I'm fine I'm gonna have an early night and hopefully I feel better tomorrow. "

" Yes you and mom are leaving early tomorrow. We'll see you in the morning mom. I'll bring Victoria home. "

Lucinda gave us both a hug and we said our goodbyes.

On the way home it was silence. I was feeling better now thank god. I have never felt so sick in all my life. I'm sure it's the bug it has to be, I mean I took the pregnancy test and it came out negative.

Im looking forward for Poland because I get to know Lucinda more, but I won't get to attached because I won't ever see her again when these months are up.

When we arrived home I went up to our room and got changed into my pyjamas and got into bed. Ace came up a few minutes later but we didn't say anything, we just went to sleep.

CHAPTER 21:Leaving Him

H ttps://www.youtube.com/watch?v=DS5ghEncSDY

When I woke up Ace was still asleep. After laying and admiring him and thinking about how mad he was last night I got up and went to the shower.

I was feeling alot better today which is great because I would hate to be nauseous and throwing up in the plane with Lucinda there with me.

I'm looking forward to hanging out with her for the time I'm with her in Poland,ive never been to Poland before so I'm looking forward to it.

When I got out of the shower I got changed into some jeans and a warm jumper.

When I was changed I went to the bathroom and put on some foundation and mascara and put on some lip gloss.

Ace was sitting on the bed on his phone dresses when I got out of the bathroom.

"Goodmorning" I said awkwardly.

"Morning "he replied," How are you feeling today? "

" I'm feeling great actually I must've just eaten something bad. "I said assuring him that I'm not pregnant.

" That's good to know" he replied. "I'm sorry about yesterday I didnt mean to be so harsh, it's just my mom told me that you could be pregnant and I believed it, ans I'm sorry If I scared you, that wasn't my intention. "

I walked over and sat down beside him on the bed. "It's okay Ace,i understand, but I assure you I'm not pregnant and I'm sorry I didn't tell you about the test but I don't see the point because it was negative."

Ace got up and got his suit jacket and put it on. "Yeah I know your not pregnant and it's fine, there was no need to tell me because your not pregnant and there was nothing to tell, now let's go because we are meeting my mom at the airport at 10. You will be flying on my private jet and my bodyguard Colin will be going with you so he can make sure you are both safe. "

" Yeah okay that's fine. "I said. I'm glad someone is coming with me and Lucinda just to make sure we are safe.

He nodded."Good, now your bags are all packed and they are ready in the car so let's go, "he said leaving the room.

I picked up my handbag and closed the door behind me.

When we arrived at the airport I saw the jet and it was huge.

Lucinda hadn't arrived yet so Ace and I waited in the car for a few minutes.

"Come on" he spoke finally. "Let's get bags ready so you can leave as soon as my mother gets here."

"Okay" I said getting out of the car and helping him with the bags. I followed Ace into the jet and he lead me to a room. I didn't know jets had rooms at least not with beds.

Ace put the bags down beside the bed and so did I and then he turned around to face me.

"You can stay in here if your tired and want to go to sleep, there's another room in the jet but it's further down, my mom can stay there" .

I nodded smiling at him. I don't know what I was thinking in that moment but I went and hugged him.

"Please be careful" I begged him.

Ace stood still surprised that I even hugged him but then he wrapped his arms around my waist and we held each other. We held each other and didn't say anything for a few short minutes Before Ace's bodyguard Massimo came in.

"Your mother is here Ace, "he said.

We let go of each other and Ace replied . "Thank you Massimo".

"Come on let's go", Ace said grabbing my hand. We intertwined our fingers and we went outside to greet Lucinda.

When we got outside Lucinda was talking with Massimo and laughing, them two must be close.

When she saw us her face lit up and she practically ran over to me and Ace.

"Hello Ace" she said pulling him into a hug causing us to let go of each other. When she let go of Ace she looked over at me and smiled.

"It's great to see you again Victoria how are you feeling today" she said giving me a hug aswell.

"It's great to see you too I'm feeling much better today I must have eaten something bad yesterday or something."

"That's great" she said." I cant wait to spend time with you in Poland we are going to have so much fun."

"I know me too, "I replied hugging her again. I genuinely couldn't wait to spend time with her despite the fact I won't ever see her again in a few months, I'm really going to miss her when I'm gone home.I don't even know if I can call it home anymore.

Lucinda and I chatted about how we're going to go shopping and go for dinner in fancy ass restaurants. They were her words exactly.

"Are you guys ready to go" Ace said coming over to us.

We both replied with "Yeah".

"Good" he said.

"See you soon Ace I love you sweetheart " Lucinda said hugging ace tightly. "I love you too mom" Ace muttered before Lucinda left to get her bags.

It was now just me and Ace staring at each other. I'll see him soon I have to.

"I'll see you soon love" Ace said staring at me. I didnt say anything I just pulled Ace in for a hug.

"I'll see you soon Ace" I whispered so that he could only hear me.

When we let go of each other we saw that Lucinda was watching us like she just witnessed a funeral,she was wiping her eyes with a tissue.

Ace turned back around and faced me.

"I love you Victoria"

"I love you Ace" I said back to him before kissing him we hugged one more time before letting go of each other.

Lucinda hugged Ace one more time before we got on the plane and left for Poland.

I can't believe Ace said he loved me,he probably only said it because Lucinda was watching us. Right...

CHAPTER 22:Ace

I can't believe I said" I love you" to Victoria, I have never said that to anyone before and I don't know why I said it. I probably just said it because my mom was watching. I dont even know.

When I got back from the airport I went to my office to get the plan ready for when the Vincenzo(spanish) mafia decide to attack. I have my warehouse ready, I have all my weapons and machinery ready to launch attack.

I was going through the underground plans of my warehouse just in case there is any spots where the Vinsenzo's could place missiles and attack us from there.

My phone started ringing and I answered it.

"What" I asked annoyed leaning back into my chair.

"Hello Ace, its certainly good to hear your voice again. "

It was Simon, the leader of the Vinsnzo mafia.

"Simon", I said getting up from my chair and grabbing a bottle of vodka.

Simon chuckled on the other end of the line before speaking again.

" As you know we are about to go into a serious situation... Now I would like to propose an offer... Think of it as a.. relief really.. Hmm, you see I have eyes watching your sweet mother and you little flower which I believe is... Victoria right, such a beautiful name,"he said through the ruffling of pa per.

I stopped moving and didn't say anything. Fuck. How does he know where they are I made sure we didn't have any eyes watching.

A second later Simon spoke again. " You see we could do a trade,you give me Victoria and I stop this war that could let's say.. get very messy for both of us and.. let's be real you don't want that do you Ace?"

I laughed and sat back down on my chair.

"Do you really think I'm going to give Victoria to you, you don't know me at all Simon do you? You must be scared that your going to die because Simon.. you know my past and I have killed alot of people and I show no mercy."

Simon scoffed on the other end of the line. " Fine no trade but just re- member this could have all been resolved, oh and I have been watching Victoria for a long time, she's very beautiful , you chose right even if its a fake marriage.. Yeah I know all about it, I'll see you soon Ace."

Shit

How does Simon know about our marriage and that its fake, it doesn't matter anyway, he will be dead soon enough and I have Colin watching Victoria and mom. Colin joined my mafia a few months ago he is very well trained so he can protect them.

The next day...

When I got up from a very sleepless night I called Colin to make sure that Victoria and my mom are safe. Colin said they are going shopping today.

I thought about yesterday and how i said goodbye to Victoria.

Its different with her but I know I can't have her.

She wants to go home and back to her old life and when she does I'll forget about her but for now I have to make sure she is safe because I would never forgive myself if something happened to her because I brought her into her life.

When I got changed into my plain black suit I went to my office to make sure I don't have any danger alerts on my computer.

Nothing

There was nothing on my computer it's weird it's too..quiet. I checked again a while later.I opened up the alert and It was a picture of a women who was tied and had tape on her mouth.

I would know her from anywhere it was Victoria.

I stared at the picture for a few seconds not being able to process that the Vinsenzos had taken Victoria.I didn't get it Colin was there with her but then it hit me Colin must be the mole. I'm gonna fucking kill him.

Victoria looks so scared, she is looking up at the celing with teary eyes. Simon must have taken this from security footage.

I called Massimo quickly to get everyone ready to attack and I went down to my weapons room and got my armour on and got my guns and put them in my back pocket.

When everyone gathered in the room I told them the plan and where everyone was situated.

"Be careful when shooting because Victoria could be there, and make sure to get her out safely. We don't have time for mistakes, everyone must be prepared for anything that could happen now let's not waste time let's go."I said quickly and sternly.

When we were on the jet to go to Spain all I thought of was Victoria and my mom. I have some of my men flying to Poland to check if my mom is there.

What if something happens to them. Their all I have,except Felix , he's my little brother but he's never here. He's in the mafia too, he's a spy. Felix gathers information from people and reports back to me.

He's spying on Victorias friend Brie at the moment making sure she doesn't go to the cops, because if she did then that would cause problems and then I would have to kill her.

Felix helped me kill Lorenzo so he's laying low for now but not for long. I'm gonna Kill Simon and get back Victoria and my mom and everything is gonna be fine.

"We've landed boss" Massimo said with his gun ready.

"Okay let's go"

I'm coming...

CHAPTER 23:Victoria

When we arrived in Poland after a long flight we went straight to Ace's penthouse and when we got there it was huge.There was wide windows looking out over Poland and you could see the people and the cars.

"Oh my god its beautiful" I said amazed looking out at the view.

Lucinda walked over beside me and looked out and smiled at the amazing view. "Isn't it, I've only ever been to Poland once but that was many years ago, I think I was in my early twenties and I was here with my friends after we were finished College and we had the best time"she said smiling.

" I'm sure you must be tired after the long trip, why don't we go and lay down for a while and then we can go shopping and go for dinner in a nice restaurant, I remember one and they had the best food, I don't know if their still open but we can give it a try" she said gathering her bags.

"Yeah we'll do that" I replied getting my bags too and making my way to my room. I was really tired and I needed to freshen up.

After getting changed into something more comfortable I got into bed and went to sleep thinking about Ace and this morning.

An hour later..

When I woke up from a much needed nap I went for a quick shower and put on some light makeup and put back on the clothes from this morning.

Lucinda was in the kitchen drinking a cup of tea when I came out of the room.

"Hi Lucinda" I said going to get myself a glass of water.

"Hello sweetheart did you get some sleep."

"Yes I did, it was much needed, did you?"

"Yes I did thank you sweetheart, now I was thinking we could go shopping first and then go for dinner."

"Yeah that's perfect" I said getting my handbag.

3 hours later...

We arrived back at the penthouse a few hours later. We both got some new clothes and we went for dinner in the restaurant she went to when she here before.

Colin came with us and carried all our bags even though we insisted.

Lucinda and I were watching 'The Notebook' on Netflix In our pj's with some Pop corn.

A while later she went to bed, so it was just me watching the movie.I stayed up for a while because I had a long nap today so I wasn't tired. I started rewatching 'The vampire diaries',I'm in love with Damon and Elena, I'm a huge Delena fan.

Colin was still awake too, he was in the kitchen on his phone texting someone.

"Here you go miss" Colin said handing me a glass of water.

"Thank you Colin but there was no need I can get it myself but thank you though" I smiled taking the glass of water from him. I continued watching my show while drinking the glass of water.

"Miss de Luca you have to come with me now, Ace is outside waiting for you" he said a few minutes later.

What? Ace is here

"How is he here I thought he had buissness to do? ", I asked confused.

"'The buissness' has been dealt with, he wants to talk to you downstairs and he wants to now, so get changed quickly and do it quitely because he only wants to speak to you" Colin said impatiently.

"Okay" I said getting up and going to my room getting changed.I was starting to feel a bit light headed but ignored it and got changed. After I got changed I met Colin in The kitchen.

"Let's go then" he said leading me to the door.I didn't even make it the door when everything went black.

https://www.youtube.com/watch?v=NW39f3t49oc

When I woke up I was in a dark room tied up, I had tape on my mouth and I started to panic. Where the hell am I.

I tried to get loose but it was no use. I kept slipping in and out of conscious-ness,a while later I heard talking and I recognised the voice it was Colin. He must have brought me here and he must have put something in my water.

I hope Lucinda is okay, I should've known this was a trick.

I started to break down, am I ever going to get out of here, what if Ace doesn't find me, what if he had something to do with this.

A few minutes later the door opened and I trembled in fear. The light beaconed the room and I saw the shadow of someone enter the room. I could barely make out their face because of how dark it was. There was only a small bit of light in the room.

"Hello Victoria, its a pleasure to finally meet you. "the stranger said.

I shivered and bowed my head. "Why am I here and who are you? "I asked sounding hourse.

My name is Simon and I'm the leader of the Spanish mafia he said, after he saw I didnt have a reaction to his little speech he spoke again.

" I see your husband didn't tell you. Ace killed someone who was going to make a very important deal with me and because Ace killed him that deal didn't happen so now he has to pay,our mafias are going to let's put it this way... War."

He must be talking about the guy Ace killed the night we went to the ball.

" What are you gonna do to me? " I asked.

" Darling I'm not going to do anything to you.. Yet. Once Ace finds out you're here he's going to come running... because I don't think he would want to get an innocent little thing killed" he said kneeling down and putting a strand of hair being my ear.

I moved away from his hand and he chuckled.

"Afterall your not really his wife this is all just a little hoaxe."

I looked up at him confused.

"How do you know? "I asked confused.

"My son Colin joined Aces mafia to get information that could be used against Ace and he found out about the contract, about your six month deal to trick his sweet mother Lucinda into believing your actually marri ed...and I must say your doing a great job."

" But anyway your what I call.. bait. He will come running I will kill him and I will have my revenge. "he said walking back and forth across the room.

All of this over a deal he must be a psychopath.

A few minutes later Colin entered the room and whispered something to the man.

Simon smiled and Colin handed him something and left the room.

" It's your lucky day sweetheart, Ace is here."

I sighed in relief. Ace came for me.

"Now before I go I'm going to give you something that will make you sleep for a while so you don't hear the commotion going on he said holding a needle.

That must be what Colin gave him. Simon moved closer to me and I tried to move away.

" Please Don't" I begged crying.

"It's alright sweetheart it will all be over soon."he said putting the needle in my arm.

A minute later my eyes felt really heavy and everything went black.

The last thing I heard was the door closing.

CHAPTER 24:In The Name Of Love

M e and my men are currently in my warehouse going over some last minute plans before entering Simon's warehouse.

I had an underground plan of his warehouse.My hacker hacked into Simon's warehouse plan, The plan showed all the rooms which gives us an advantage.

"He must be keeping Victoria underground in one of the rooms", I said pointing to the rooms on the lay out sheet.

" So we have to get in there safely, so be careful, we don't know what type of weapons they have. We could be walking straight into a trap and we could be gunned down so we have to be careful."

Everyone was gathering there weapons when my phone started ringing.

It's probably Simon.

"What?" I asked.

" Hello Ace, I heard about you going into a fight with the Spanish mafia, I'm Luca the leader of the Sicilian mafia" he said.

"Okay, why are you calling me I have stuff to do? "I said impatiently.

" I'm aware that Simon is keeping your wife Victoria captive."

" How do you know that"? I asked confused.

"I have someone on the inside gathering info to take him down,me and Simon are enemies too and I have been trying to take him down for years but I've never had the chance,I was thinking me and you could take him down together and end this, I have advanced weapons and I know every room so we could have an advantage."

" Okay fine come to my warehouse and be quick we don't have long", I said hanging up.

I went back in to the warehouse and everyone gathered around.

"Luca the leader of the Sicilian mafia is coming here with his men and he is helping us take Simon and his mafia down, he has someone on the inside so Luca knows the rooms and what weapons they have. It's our best chance at finding Victoria and getting her out safely" I said.

Everyone nodded and a few minutes later Luca and his men were here.

"Hello Ace its good to finally meet you" he said shaking my hand.

"You too, now let's get down to it, we need to be out of there by nightfall"I said going over to the table showing Luca and his men the layout.

https://www.youtube.com/watch?v=l7hHeZa3BYU

A few minutes later..

After a few minutes everyone knew the plan and we were ready to go.

We went on the helicopter to get there faster,Luca went on his own helicopter and we were there in a few minutes. We landed minutes away from Simon's warehouse so he won't see us coming.

When we surrounded the warehouse we made our move and just as I suspected we were walking straight into a trap.

Guns went off and everyone started shooting.

When I entered the warehouse I killed who ever I saw and made my way to the basement door.

When I looked down it was very quiet, Luca and a few of my men came with me.

"Simon is hiding here somewhere" I said opening every door looking for Victoria.

"Yeah he'll be here somewhere", Luca said checking his surroundings.

I'm coming love, just hold on a little longer.

After a few minutes of looking in every room I heard talking on the other end of one the doors.

I beckoned Luca and my men and I kicked the door open and it was no other then Colin and Simon and another person,he loosened up when he saw Luca so I'm guessing he's the inside man.

Simon was sitting in a chair and Colin was standing behind him. Simon was surprised when he saw Luca.

"It's a pleasure to see you again Ace and Luca I'm surprised to see you here."

"Where's Victoria, Simon? " I ordered.

"Don't worry she's safe... For now."

"Simon I swear to god give me Victoria or I will give you the worst death imaginable" I said impatiently.

"Really" he said laughing looking at Colin.

I looked at Luca and he was just as pissed off.

Simon went back to his desk and sat down on his chair, he grabbed a gun from under his desk and shot me in the arm.My men started shooting at Colin and Simon.

I groaned in pain and Luca started shooting and so did the inside man.I shot Colin in the forehead and Luca shot Simon straight in the heart.

"That was easier then I expected" Luca said taken aback," It's good to see you again Elijah "Luca said.

" It was too easy" I said.

"It's not easy it's Simon plan, there are bombs about to go off, he has them everywhere in the building, so we need to find my sister now" Elijah said.

"Shit, go and tell everyone and I'll find Victoria" I said leaving to find Victoria.

"Okay but be quick you only have a few minutes tops" Elijah said.

"Okay" I said running down the hall looking for Victoria.

This song reminds me of the situation..

https://www.youtube.com/watch?v=1zjvX5W04VI

The hall came to a dead end and there was one door left and it was locked. I kicked it open and I saw Victoria laying there on the floor unconscious tied up.

I ran over to her" Victoria I'm here"I said trying to wake her

"Ace" she mumbled her eyes closing and opening.

"I've got you love" I said untieing her and picking her up.

I made my way back up to the warehouse with Victoria in my arms as fast as I could and Luca, Elijah and my men were waiting.

"OK let's go" Luca shouted and everyone made their way outside to the helicopters.

When we were up in the air the warehouse exploded. I looked down at Victoria who was laying in my lap still unconscious.

"We're going to the airport,I have a doctor waiting and I need to get Victoria medical care to check that shes alright."I said.

"Yeah do, I need to go home to my wife and son and my men need some medical care too, a few got shot but their going to be fine. Elijah you can stay if you want, I'm sure you want to spend time with Victoria when she wakes up.

"Yes thank you boss" Elijah said looking at Victoria worriedly.

A while later...

When we landed Luca left on his own private jet with his men and me, Elijah and Victoria went on mine.

I had two doctors waiting on the jet when we arrived. The doctor told me he had to do some blood tests on Victoria to see if there is anything wrong with her.

I got my arm stitched up and Elijah was tended to aswell and waited for the doctor to give me some news on Victoria.One of my men called from Poland and told me that my mom was Okay, she's waiting at home for me and Victoria to come back. I was worried about Victoria, please be okay I don't know what I will do if she isn't okay I would never forgive myself.

CHAPTER 25:Shocking News

While waiting for the doctor to give me Victoria's test results Elijah told me how he was Victoria's older brother. He joined Luca's mafia to pay off some family debt but that meant he couldn't contact Victoria for safety issues.

"I haven't seen her in seven years" Elijah said looking out the window.

My eyes widened "Seven years, that's a long time" I said.

"Yeah it is, I was all she had left and I abandoned her", Elijah said shaking his head.

"What do you mean you abandoned her" I asked confused.

He walked over to the table and got a glass of tequila and sat across form me. " Our parents died in a car accident when we were younger and we stayed with our aunt till I was 18 and Victoria was 16 and then our aunt died of a heart attack so I had to look after Victoria myself, but our family had alot of gambling debt and then Luca came looking for me and I had to join his mafia, he was really bad at first, a few times I thought he was gonna kill me but he's alot nicer now seen as he has his son and his wife" he said chuckling.

I chuckled too "She's going to be fine Elijah" I said.

"Yeah I know I just feel guilty for leaving her all alone", he said.

The doctor came towards us with a clipboard in his hand. "Mr De Luca I have you wife's blood test results if you want to come with me."

"Okay" I said getting up from my chair. I nodded at Elijah and he let out a small smile.

When we arrived in the room I saw Victoria laying there on the bed with an IV in her arm.

"I just want to say your wife is okay before we get started".

I let out a sigh of relief.

"She was injected with a sedative which is why she is unconscious but she will wake up in a few hours. "

I nodded. Thank God she is okay I don't know what I would do if she wasn't.

"She was lucky it wasn't anything stronger as it would have affected the pregnancy".

What??

"What do you mean Pregnancy?" I asked .

The doctor's face tensed up in confusion at the question.

" Oh... I guess you didn't know, Victoria is pregnant, about 5 to 8 weeks it seems" he said looking through the clipboard in his hand.

Victoria's pregnant, but how she took a test and it came back negative.

"No, there must be a mistake, she took a pregnancy test and it came back negative"

"False results can happen, it's rare but it happens", the doctor said walking over beside to where Victoria is laying.

"Look, I can do a scan when your wife wakes up to show you the results? "he asked.

"Yeah do it now" I ordered walking over beside the bed to where Victoria is.

"It might be too early but hopefully we can find the heartbeat" he said turning on the machine.

The doctor pulled up Victoria's shirt and put on some sort of gel, when he put it on her stomach she moved a little.

It took a while finding the heartbeat but the doctor found it eventually.

"There's the heartbeat" he said and the sound filled the room.

I smiled at the sound before the doctor spoke again.

"Wait... hold on" he said moving the thing on Victorias stomach around.

"What is it? "I asked worried. I looked on the machine and saw two blobs.

" Congratulations Mr de Luca, you're having twins" he said pointing to the blobs on the screen.

Twins, I'm going to be a dad to twins.

"Here's the second heartbeat" the doctor said and the second heartbeat filled the room.

A few minutes later..

After learning that I'm going to be a dad I was shocked. I sat beside the bed holding Victoria's hand waiting for her to wake up.

A half an hour later Victoria started to wake up.

"Ace? "she mumbled

" Hello love"

CHAPTER 26: The Future

"Hello love"

It was Ace. He was sitting beside me on a bed holding my hand.

"Hi" I whispered.

"How are you feeling? "he asked.

" Good, just really tired." I said.

It feels like I haven't slept in days and my entire body aches.

Ace smiled" I have to tell you something, love. "

" Okay". I said sitting up from my lying position wondering what he was going to say.

"The doctor said your fine and that Simon gave you a strong sedative which will ware off in a few hours and"....He hesitated closing his eyes..." Your pregnant".

I didnt say anything for a moment. I'm pregnant. I can't believe it but how, I just took a pregnancy test and it was negative.

I laughed until I saw the seriousness on his face. "What? But... How..The pregnancy test was negative."

"I know,the doctor said it was a false result. "he said standing up and going to a table and pouring me a glass of water.

He handed me the glass of water. " The doctor did a scan and it seems you are 5 to 8 weeks pregnant...We're having twins Victoria.. I heard the heartbeats."

Twins.

" Twins". I whispered smiling putting my hand to my stomach.

How did I not know, I mean the night Ace and I had dinner with Lucinda I was really sick and I have never been that sick... Ever.

"What does this mean for us? "I asked averting my eyes back to his.

" What do you mean?" he asked confused.

" The Deal, the six month contract, what does this mean for us.. Are we going to stay together until I give birth or... "I didn't say the rest hoping he would figure it out.

He didn't say anything which is a bad sign, he looked out the plane window with his hands in his suit pockets.

"The deal stays the same but it will be delayed of course until you have the babies and then you can go home and I will come to visit the babies when ever I can."He said and left the room.

I started tearing up but blinked them away. I should have known his feelings weren't real, they were never real. I started reminiscing every moment we had. I love him, I love Ace de Luca, the ruthless mafia leader that I feared and hated for taking me from my life and Brie.

He just used me as an allibi...

https://www.youtube.com/watch?v=9z9vNHWMHOg

While trying to hold myself together there was a knock on the door, it's probably Ace I thought, so I didn't say anything. The door opened and it was the last person I ever expected to see.

It was Elijah, my big brother who I havent seen since I was 16.

We didnt say anything, we just stared at each other not quite believing we were reunited after all this time.

"Elijah" I said crying.

"Hey sis". Elijah said coming to the bed and sitting down and pulling me into a hug.

"Your here, I thought I'd never see you again."I said not wanting to let go of him.

" I'm sorry I left,I had no choice but I'm here now and I'm never leaving you again."Elijah said letting go of me.

I wiped my tears and we were both laughing.

" Where have you been" I said holding his hand after we calmed down.

"I've been working for The Sicillian mafia. "

"What? The Sicillian mafia. Why? "I asked.

" Our family had alot of gambling debt Victoria and the leader of the mafia, Luca came looking for me and told me he owned the casinos, he said if I didn't join and work for him he'd kill us."

" Oh my god Elijah" I said.

"Don't worry he's way nicer then he was, he has a child and a wife now. "

"Do you have to go back"? I asked worriedly.

"I have to, but him and Ace joined together today and saved you. I will never leave you again Victoria. I promise."

"Ace told me your pregnant, I'm going to be an uncle". He said smiling.

"I'm having Twins Elijah, your gonna have two niece's or nephews or your going to have a niece and nephew."I said laughing.

" How are you feeling" Elijah asked.

"I'm feeling..Good just tired, but really happy" I said pulling him in for another hug.

"I'll go to the chef to get you some food, after all your feeding for three, and there's clothes there"he said putting the clothes on the bed.

" We're going to be landing soon aswell". He said.

" Thanks Elijah." I said.

As he was about to leave I called him back.

"Elijah, where's the doctor? "

I wanted to hear the heartbeats of my babies and see them on the screen.

"He's outside,Why? Are you feeling unwell? "he asked worriedly coming to my side.

" No I'm feeling fine, it's just Ace said he heard the heartbeats and I want to hear them."

" Okay I'll get him now. "Elijah said leaving.

Not even a minute later the doctor came in.

" How are you feeling, Ms De Luca" the doctor said.

"I'm feeling fine, thank you, would you mind if you did a scan it's just I'm dying to hear the heatbeats." I said.

"No problem". He said putting gloves on and turning on the machine.

"Thank you." I said laying down.

"This might be a little cold" he said applying the gel on my stomach.

I moved a little under the cold touch of the gel,I looked up at the machine and then saw the two little blobs.

"There they are" he said pointing to them on the screen.

"Here are the heartbeats" he said turning up the machine.

I saw the lines go up and down on the screen and the sound filled my ears. I smiled taking in this moment.

A few minutes later the doctor turned off the machine and gave me a tissue to wipe my stomach.

"Thank you" I said sitting up.

He sat on the chair beside the bed with a clipboard in his hand. "Now your around 5 to 8 weeks pregnant.Mr De Luca told me you took a pregnancy test a few weeks ago and it came back negative."

I nodded.

"Your symptoms over the next few months are going to be tiredness, morning sickness, cravings and some mood swings."

"Okay" I said taking all the information in.

"Here's the list of foods you should eat so the babies get the right amount of nutrients and you of course,and here's the foods you need to avoid." he said handing me the list.

"Thank you "I said.

" No problem" he said. _______________________________________

When the doctor left the room I got changed into a comfy outfit and made a promise to myself and my babies, that I will always protect them, no matter what.

After I got changed Elijah brought me some food and we talked about the years we spent apart and then we landed.

CHAPTER 27: Denial

I love her.

I love Victoria. The woman I saw in the nightclub, who was in the pretty red dress, dancing with her friend. I took her to be my pretend wife so my mother would lay off my back. Now she's carrying my children.

Shit

How did I let it get this far, I should have buried the deal the second I started having feelings for her.

____

When I told her that she was pregnant, just for one split second I thought we could be a normal family but we can't.

I already put her in danger because I'm in the mafia. I've become too weak, and I can't be weak.

When I told her the deal remains the same I wasn't lying, she will go home when she has had our kids and I will provide her with 24 hour security.

I will visit every few days to see them and it will be fine.

I'll get over her. I have to.

When we landed I saw Victoria and Elijah laughing. Maybe she isn't as upset as i thought she was. Hmm.

When we arrived home a while later, Victoria and I exchanged a quick glance but she quickly looked away.

It's good to be home.

"Do you want something to eat Victoria,you must be hungry after the long drive" . Elijah said going to the kitchen.

"No I'm fine, I'm just gonna have a bath and go to bed I'm still pretty tired."Victoria said hugging Elijah.

" Okay, goodnight call me if you need anything"Elijah said.

" OK, goodnight" she muttered on her way to the stairs.

I left to go to the spare room because I needed to give Victoria her space and I needed it if I'm ever gonna get over her. My phone started ringing asn it was Felix. I haven't heard from him in a while.Its probably news about Brie. He's being spying on Brie since I took Victoria, Knowing Felix he's probably fucking her aswell as spying on her.

"What" I said taking off my tie.

What's up brother, its been awhile since we've talked but I've been watching Victoria's friend Brie and she hasn't said anything to anyone, but anyways I followed her into a club and she saw me and she knows I've been watching her for months.

I sighed in annoyance and sat down on my bed.

"Fucksake Felix, you had one Goddamn job, watch the friend and make sure she didn't say anything, what are you doing now."

He had ONE job.

"I'm in her apartment, she's at work right now." Felix said chucking on the other line.

I'm gonna kill him, I swear to god.

"Why are you in her apartment? don't tell me you fucked her".

"Why do you think so low of me brother, what makes you think I fucked her."

"Felix did you fuck her."

"Okay yes I did, but it was only because I was so horny,then we started meeting up and we're kind of going out now.

Great.

"You know what Felix". I said rubbing my forehead fed up with this conversation,"Come home tomorrow and bring the friend, Victoria needs the company and I have to tell you and mom something.

There was silence on the other end of the line for a few seconds.

" Hmm wasn't expecting that but sure okay see you then."

I ended the call before he could say anything else. I went for a cold shower and went to bed.

When I left to go upstairs I went for a long nice bath and went straight to bed and watched a little bit of Netflix. I was waiting for Ace to come in but he never did, he's probably in the spare room.When I go home when the babies are born i won't be seeing him everyday and I will get over him and my feelings for him will be a distant memory.

The next day...

When I woke up I went straight to the shower and put on a nice outfit. I might go shopping today and spend some time with Elijah and besides I need to start buying some baby clothes.

CHAPTER 28:Reunited

When I finished getting ready I went down to the kitchen and Elijah was there eating some toast and drinking tea. I was prepared for the awkward exchanged glances with Ace but he wasn't there, he's probably in his office.

"Goodmorning. "I said to Elijah happily getting some coffee.

" Morning". He said sleepily.

I sat down beside him on the chair. "Do you want to come shopping with me"? I asked hopefully.

I want to spend as much time with him as I can before he has to go back to Sicily,and besides I need to get out of the house.

"You know I hate shopping Tori ".

He knows I hate being called Tori. Our mom gave that nickname to me and it just stuck, my mom gave Elijah a nickname aswell and he hated it.

I groaned "Come on 'Eli' we need to spend time together before you go back to Sicily".

He smirked" I told you not to call me that but fine I'll go with you but let me have a quick shower first. "

"And I told you not to call me Tori, you know I hate that nickname but Yes! thank you I promise you won't regret it and we can go to McDonald's aswell I know you used to love it."

"Yes! Now I definitely can't refuse" Elijah said before going upstairs to shower.

I can't wait to get out of the house, I just have to tell Ace first just so he knows I'm safe, and I will probably need security with me. So after my coffee I made my way to Ace's office.

I closed my eyes and brought my hand to the door. I knocked on the door and there was no reply. I opened the door and Ace was sitting at his desk going through some paperwork.

He looked up at me and muttered a "goodmorning". His eyes went up and down as he viewed my body,I ignored the butterflies in my stomach and sat down in front of his desk.

"Good morning. "

"How are you feeling today?"he asked sinking back into his chair.

" I'm feeling fine thank you, Umm-I was just coming to tell you that I'm going shopping with Elijah for awhile".

"No your not".

I squinted my eyes at him In anger. " What do you mean 'no your not' "?

"No your not as in your carrying my children and you need to be safe, I will send Aubrey to get anything you need -or you know what you can just have my card and you can shop online, you have better fashion sense then Aubrey anyway. "

"So that's all I am then" I said shaking my head" I'm just the woman carrying your children.? "

"What's that supposed to mean?"

" You know what I mean". I said as a tear came running down my eye.

He knows just as well as I do all the things we did and all the laughs we shared. He couldn't of just turned his feelings off overnight could he? When I met his eyes his face relaxed and he took his hand and covered his mouth.

"Look Victoria I don't know what you want me to say, I need you to stay safe because I have just got you got back from Simon and you want to go shopping. Are you trying to put yourself in danger on purpose so I can save you or are you really that stupid to know you could get yourself killed if one of my enemies follows you and takes you or worse kills you? "

" I will have Elijah with me and I will have security, you just want to keep me here so I have to see you everywhere I go!"I said getting up to leave,but before I could even leave Ace blocked the door. How did he even get there so fast??

"Ace ju-"

" What do you mean I'm doing this so you have to see me"?He said cutting me off trapping me between the door and him with his arms at the side of my head.

"You know why Ace, you know my feelings towards you and you want me to pack up and leave when our kids are born and go home, and then what..

We're going to be strangers and the only thing we will have connecting us are our children."

"And I'll never be able to stop loving you if I have to see you everyday.. So please Ace just leave me alone.. Please".

https://www.youtube.com/watch?v=EJt51BOGb-o

A/N I'm doing this song from Victoria's point of view on how Ace is denying his feelings towards her.

*

I closed my eyes and leaned my head back onto the door trying to hold back the tears.

"Victoria you know what I am, I'm a mafia leader you and our kids will always be in danger."

I closed my eyes tighter because I know he's right.I know me and my kids will always be in danger but we're going to be in more danger without him right?

I fell in love with an emotionless guy that could kill you without showing any remorse. I thought he was evil when he took me but I got to know him and he's everything but.Hes much more then a mafia leader.

I opened my eyes to look at him. "I know Ace. I know who I fell in love with, I know you have many enemies out there, but your not what you portray Ace your much more then that and you need to know that,your not evil Ace and you deserve to be happy, Your not your father Ace."

He doesn't say anything he just looks blankly at me.

"Come here". He said pulling me in for a hug. I buried my head into his neck and we stayed there for a few seconds before he pulled me away from him but he was still holding my waist. Our faces were inches apart and I looked down at his lips in temptation but I brought myself back to his eyes.

For the next few seconds we just stared into eachothers eyes.He looked into my eyes and I could see the temptation and then he pulled me closer and kissed me roughly.

I kissed him back and wrapped my hands around his neck and he picked me up and put my legs round his waist. He brought me to his desk and sat me down on it, and he stood between my legs.

"Fuck" he groaned into my mouth when I pulled him closer with my legs still wrapped around his waist and I could feel his bulge against me,I let out a small moan at the touch.

"I want you to touch me" I begged pulling away.

He smiled before pulling my dress up and gliding his hands up my thighs. He touched my panties and my core was throbbing wanting more.

A part of me is saying leave! But I just want his touch---I need him to touch me. Ace moved my panties to the side and stroked my pussy before pinching my bud and without warning he put two fingers in. I moaned burying my head into his neck.

"Do you like that, love?"

"Yes" I moaned into his neck. I felt a build up of pressure in my stomach when he reached my g-spot,he started increasing his speed and I pulled away from his his neck and kissed him.

I raised my head back while I came all over his fingers. He took his fingers out and layed his forehead against mine,he layed his hand on my stomach and smiled, I layed my hand on his and we stayed like that for the next minute and then there was a knock on the door.

"One second" Ace shouted while pulling himself away from me and grabbing me a tissue to wipe my legs, I got off the table and adjusted my dress and my hair and went over to Ace.

"We're going to be okay Ace, we have you protecting us" I said assuring him.

"What if it isn't enough" he whispered and pulled me in for a hug, He held me tight like I would disappear if he let me go.

"Come on" he said "I have a surprise waiting for you." he said taking my hand and walking us to the door.

This moment felt perfect and I don't want it to end..

CHAPTER 29: Till Death Do Us Part

"I have a surprise for you".

I took Ace's hand and we went downstairs. When we reached the bottom of the stairs I saw Elijah and Felix. What is Felix doing here?

I looked at Ace with confusion and he had a smug look on his face. I looked back towards the kitchen and a woman steeped out. I would recognise her anywhere. It was Brie.

I let go of Ace's hand and ran to Brie and hugged her so hard. Ace muttered a "Victoria be careful" and came over to the kitchen and greeted Felix and my brother.

"Oh my god Brie, what are you doing here?"I asked quite not believing my best friend was here.

" I'm here to see my best friend of course,I've missed you so much". She said pulling me in for a hug.

"Hi Felix its great to see you again".I said going over and hugging him.

"You too Victoria,it's been a while since I saw you last, how are you and my brother getting on?" he asked.

I thought back to few moments ago when we were in his office. I don't know if that was the spur of the moment or does he feel something for me, I know he feels he won't be able to protect me and out children but we are going to be safe.

" I'll let Ace tell you about that, I'm going to catch up with Brie." I said avoiding the question because I don't know what to say.

"Yeah, we need to catch up and besides we're going shopping to get some clothes and we can leave the men to do what ---mafia people--do I suppose." Brie said coming to my side.

I chuckled be for looking at Ace. "Would it be okay if we went shopping?"

He hesitated for a moment but then nodded. "Fine ye can go but you will be bringing security for your safety." he said.

"Yes! "Brie screamed and went over to Felix. Their totally together.I went over to Ace and hugged him goodbye.

"Thank you" I whispered.

"Please be careful and don't let Brie use up all the money on my credit card." he said into my ear. I laughed into his neck and stopped hugging him but I kept my arms around his neck.

"I will and I won't." I looked over at Brie and Felix and there hugging and Elijah is looking like a lost puppy.

"There dating aren't they" I whispered to Ace looking at Felix and Brie.

"Yeah they are, I sent him to spy on her and look at whats happened."

"You sent him to spy on her,you know what I'm honestly not surprised." I said laughing.

"Okay Vic let's go I'm starving" Brie said coming over.

" Okay" I said looking at her and then back to Ace "Bye" I whispered before letting him go.

"Bye". He replied smiling leaning against the door.

"Bye Elijah, you got off shopping with me this time, see you soon, oh and do you still want that McDonald's?" I asked going to hug him.

"Haha yess please." Elijah said.

"Okay bye, bye Felix." I said leaving.

"Bye Victoria." Felix said hugging Brie one more time. I went over to Brie and then we went to the car with our security guards.

*

"So how have you been? Brie asked

" It's been good, really good, Umm I'm pregnant."I said getting straight to the point.

Brie's face dropped" WHAT YOUR PREGANT!?"

" I know its weird, I'm having twins."I said with tears in my eyes.

"Oh my god Vic, I'm so happy for you.Im going to be an aunt, I can't believe it". She said crying aswell.

"Now tell me about you, what have you been up to the last few months?"

"Well, a few days after you called me to tell me you were taken by Ace, Felix started following me and spying on me and then I caught him in this club and then we basically hooked up again,he was the guy I went home with that night we went to the club and we spent time together for a while and then he asked me to be his girlfriend."

" That was him?" I asked shocked. "I knew it, you guys looked really cosy, oh Brie I'm so happy for you." I said pulling her in for a hug.

"I missed you so much Brie."

"I missed you too Vic."

https://www.youtube.com/watch?v=8zkoJWZEtoE

A few hours later we were done shopping, we talked a lot about the last few months and I told her about the situation with Ace. Right now we were on the way home.

"How long are you staying"? I asked. I hope she stays for a while, I missed her company so much.

"I took a few weeks off so a few weeks maybe."

Brie works in a cafe, her parents run to and it's very successful.

"That's great Brie, it'll be great to have you."

*

A while later we arrived home and when we went inside everyone was sitting around the table and Lucinda was there aswell.

"Hi everyone."Brie and I said when we came in.

I looked over at Ace and he smiled at me and he got up and came over to me and hugged me.

" I told mom and Felix about the pregnancy so be prepared for a million questions." he whispered in my ear before kissing me on the lips.

"Hi Brie it's lovely to meet you, I'm Lucinda, Felix's mom."

"Oh my god hi Lucinda it's great to meet you". Brie said going in for a hug.

I gave Elijah his McDonald's and he said "Thank you "before devouring his burger.

I went and sat down on Ace's lap and he wrapped his hand around my stomach, I'm four months pregnant now, only five months left until we meet our angels.

"Hello sweetheart, it's great to know your safe I'm sorry I couldn't do anything to save you from Colin" . Lucinda said coming over and I got up from Ace's lap to hug her.

"No there was nothing you could have done anyway, we're both safe and that's the main thing."

"You mean four,Ace told us about the pregnancy, congratulations I'm so happy for you guys I'm gonna be a grandmother."she said laughing.

" Thank you Lucinda" I said hugging her one more time and sitting back on Ace's lap.

"Come up to the office I need to talk to you." he said whispering in my ear.

"Okay. " I whispered.

"We'll be back soon we just need to talk" . He said leading me upstairs.

---

https://www.youtube.com/watch?v=GLqsAC7qSfI

A/N This song suits this moment alot.

When we got to his office Ace closed the door behind him and then he kissed me.I kissed him back ans wrapped my legs around his waist.He sat me carefully on the desk and hled me close.

"I love you Victoria. I have loved you from the moment I saw you in that club and I don't ever want to live without you and I will promise to always protect you and our kids. I love you."

He loves me.

"I love you Ace, and I dont ever want to live without you. Does this mean we're officially husband and wife?"

"Yes, wife. "he said smiling before kissing me again.

I muttered" I love you husband".

"I love you too wife" he said in my mouth.

I can't believe this is happening. We're officially husband and wife and I can't believe it.

We stared at each other for the next minute before Ace spoke again.

"Till Death Do Us Part, Victoria De luca."

I smiled.

"Till Death Do Us Part, Ace De Luca."

CHAPTER 30:New Type Of Love

A few months later...

It's been a few month's since Ace and I confessed our feelings towards each other. We're officially husband and wife and I'm ecstatic. It's never how I imagined it would be, it's even better. When I was younger I always dreamed of finding my Prince charming and I've found him.

Our love story wasn't the most normal but I wouldn't change a thing. I'm almost 9 months pregnant now and I can't wait to meet my angels. We did a gender reveal and we're having a boy and a girl. Ace was so excited when we found out, and so was I.

We just can't wait to meet them.

It's just me and Ace in our house. Elijah had to go back to the Sicillian mafia but Luca said he was free to leave whenever but Elijah didnt want to.

Elijah has a girlfriend who is in the Sicillian mafia aswell. Her name is Rya, she's an assassin and a very good one at that.

Rya and Elijah are engaged and expecting their first child, it's a girl. I can't wait to be an aunt and Elijah is so excited to be a father.

Felix and Brie left the same time Elijah did, they only live a few minutes away. Brie and Felix got married a few days ago. Everyone's so in love and I'm here for it.

https://www.youtube.com/watch?v=7rINKu7Dra4

Ace and I have a photo shoot today and I can't wait. I'm currently doing my makeup in the bedroom and Ace just got out of thr shower.

"Hey wife". Ace said coming out in nothing but a towel.

I turned around and stood up "Hey husband",giving him a kiss. He groaned and pulled me in tighter.

"You look beautiful, love".

"Thank you, you do aswell if I must say so myself" I said eyeing his entire body and giving him a kiss.

"Luca texted me and was wondering if we could all join together after the babies are born and have a barbecue, he's going to bring his wife and his son and the entire mafia so Elijah and Rya will be coming aswell. "he said with his hands wrapped around my waist.

"That sounds great, I miss Elijah and it would be great to see him and Rya and Felix and Brie must come aswell and you need to invite Massimo and the rest of your mafia aswell". I said with my shoulders wrapped around his shoulders.

I groaned in pain when the babies kicked and layed my head on Ace's shoulders.

"Are you okay, love?" Ace asked worriedly.

"Yeah it's just the baby's kicking my internal organs". I said laughing through the pain.

Ace layed his hand on my stomach and they stopped kicking straight away.

"Really? They stopped kicking as soon as you put your hand on my stomach." I layed my head onto Aces shoulders and laughed.

"They love me already." Ace said grinning from ear to ear, like a chesire cat.

The photoshoot picture...